Paul Milenski

1990

Best Wishes

SEXUAL
RHYTHMS

PAUL MILENSKI *&* MARILYN GRANDE

SEXUAL

RHYTHMS

SUDDEN FICTIONS

Mountain Press • *Williamstown, MA*

The text of this book is composed in Palatino, with display type
set in Zapf Chancery and Eras Medium. Typography by the
STI Group, Inc., Pittsfield, MA; printing by Eagle Printing, Pittsfield, MA

COVER ART AND BOOK DESIGN
BY JULIO GRANDA

First Edition
Library of Congress Catalog Card Number: 90-61106

ISBN 0-9625313-0-8

Mountain Press
Stratton Hills
Williamstown, MA 01267

1 2 3 4 5 6 7 8 9 0

ACKNOWLEDGMENTS

THE AUTHORS THANK editors Susan Richardson, CA-LYPSO, El Cajon, CA, and Ron Fleshman, READ ME, Everett, WA, for publishing some of the stories previous to their printing here; Peter Drozd and Cal Joppru of The Reproshop for assistance; and also the Massachusetts Arts Lottery Councils of Pittsfield and Northern Berkshire for their generous assistance in support of this project.

For Those We Love:

Philip, Stuart, Beverly, Aaron, Kate,
Tomas Cat, and Special Friends.

Contents

SEXUAL
RHYTHMS

The Velvet Room

WHEN HE CALLED, she said she was living on Hoxey Street with a girlfriend. He knew the house; it was a large converted colonial, a little tacky, white with purple trim. He parked on the street, walked up the long walk, pulled open a heavy door. The mailboxes in the hall read Jones & Carroll 2-A. When he knocked, he could hear her footsteps before she opened the door.

As always, she looked glorious, dark-skinned, sable-haired, tall and thin. She wore sneakers and jeans, and a man's work shirt—braless.

She didn't give him a hug or kiss, but she smiled. "Hello, Frank," she said.

"Hello, Jane."

"Come on, come on in."

He followed, through the kitchen, to the living room.

"Here we go, Frank." She indicated a velvet easy chair in a purple room with velvet drapes and lamp shades and scatter rugs. She sat across from him on a purple velvet sofa; she crossed her long legs.

He looked around. The room was oppressive, as though the color and fabric were extracting oxygen, thinning the air.

"So this is where you live?"

"Ahuh."

"I mean, it looks comfortable, very warm."

"Margaret and I like it. We have fun here."

"I don't know Margaret."

"I met her at work. She's crazy."

He looked around the room; it was not small but appeared so, the walls, ceiling, and floor converging in a purple velvet haze.

"What made you call, Frank?"

This is why he liked her, why he loved her really— she was direct and honest.

"I wanted to see you."

"What for, Frank?"

"I'm confused . . . I guess it's just that I'm confused."

She rose and walked over to him. She was dark, her skin, her hair; she was very sexy. She focused in on him with her big dark eyes. "What do you want, Frank?"

"Well, ah . . . God, Jane, I don't know. I mean—"

"What do you want to drink, Frank?"

He asked for a beer. She got up, went to the kitchen. While she was gone, he studied the room. It bothered him. The velvet was one thing, but the purple, that bothered him more. Outside trim, inside the same tackiness—God!

She returned with two Molsons, wiped off the mouth of hers, sat with her legs over one end of the sofa, drank right out of the bottle. She was unpretentious, incredibly spontaneous, sexy.

"Good beer," he said.

"Friends leave it."

"What's that?"

"Friends leave the beer."

"Oh."

"You know me, Frank. I wouldn't know what to

buy."

"Oh, sure . . . yes, Jane."

She sipped from her beer, stared at him as she drank. It was years; he had not seen anyone sexier. Not in New York. Not in Boston. Her thinness and tallness made her look vogueish, sophisticated.

"So what are you confused about, Frank?"

"Jesus, God, Jane, the bedroom isn't purple too, is it?"

"You like the color, Frank? Really, do you like it?"

"It's warm . . . It's comfortable."

"Margaret and I keep picking up pieces. Did you notice the outside? The outside is purple."

"I noticed."

"Great idea, huh, outside, inside?"

"I imagine it probably is."

"Margaret and I have a lot of fun here, just living, you know. We have friends over, cook, party . . . decorate."

Her hair fell back from one ear; a small gold stud glistened. She had perfect ears. Physically, there was nothing about her he didn't like. She had thin arms, little feet; she had wispy little sideburns. And, she was honest.

"I tried, didn't I, Frank?"

"You did more than try, Jane. You did more than that."

"I tried very hard."

"Yes, you did."

"So, it's been a long time. I mean, there's things gone by, you know."

"I imagine so."

"You were confused before, you know. You were the

one confused."

"Yes, I was."

"I'm pretty happy, Frank. I mean, I'm just living, nothing complicated."

"You're happy."

"Yes, Frank, I am."

She smiled. Her beauty seemed so out of place. It didn't make sense, the room and her. But there was always something like this. Some purple thing. Some velvet thing.

"I guess I like the room, Jane, and the house. I mean, Jesus Christ, it's you."

"Thanks, Frank," she said. "Thank you."

Now she was smiling broadly, lighting up the place, just being herself. Beautiful. Honest. He loved her; that was honest, too.

But now he had to leave her again. He had to. And he'd have to do it like velvet, because he was the one who started it again, he could see that, and he'd have to finish it. God, she was beautiful! She was a godamn beautiful person. Anyone else and he wouldn't have lasted as long as he did. When he left, he promised himself, he'd blink his eyes, he wouldn't look inside or outside, he'd just leave, drive away.

The Velvet Room

*Y*OU'RE STIFF!" he pronounced emphatically, handing the camera to his assistant.

"I . . . the model began while shading her eyes from the bright lights in front of her, searching for the owner of the voice.

"You look great, babe. But the moves are duds. What's it gonna take, hmmm?" His voice was low and resonant but with an edge of exasperation. "Should we give her a red?" he mumbled to someone near him.

"Maybe it's the music," she tried. "I love to dance, but I'm not really into rap." She paced back and forth, just out of reach of the lights—measured steps, alone with her thoughts.

"Hold the music," he shouted.

"What you're not into is this shoot, hon," observed the tall, thin woman who leaned in the corner shadows, a notebook in hand. "Modeling is more than a pretty face and body." She lit a cigarette.

"Well, I'm trying," the girl murmured, turning around a couple of times to sink and sit Indian style on the floor, pulling her long legs in close. She put her face in her hands, her long hair sliding down each side of her like a curtain.

"Shit," she whispered.

"Hand me my camera, Ann," he said to his assistant. "Needle her—keep it up. She's losing rigidity in her despair."

"What the . . . "Ann began.

"Just hand me the fucking camera," he growled.

The model looked up startled. Click.

"What's going on?" she asked softly, shaking her head back, her hair spraying out to settle against her tilted neck and shoulder.

"Shut up and figure it out," he yelled to her. "Can you hear me?" he hissed to Ann. "Find some Gerry Mulligan or Billie Holliday. Get on it!"

"I'm not sure what you want . . . " the model started. Click.

"It all started with your parents selling you to us," he intoned, slowly.

She began to stand up, one arm pushing herself up, the other hand holding back her hair. Click.

"Barbara," the model pleaded to the woman in the corner, "I don't want to be here."

"Too late," was her answer, as Barbara left through a door that slammed shut.

The girl stood tall, her fingers fanned out by her sides, her shoulders shrugged.

"My parents only want what's best for . . . "

"Fuck that!" he yelled, laughing eerily. Click.

"Maybe I'm only fourteen, but I know what you're trying to . . . "

"You know nothing, doll, or you wouldn't be here."

Tears began to spill down her face. Click.

"Where's the music?" he hissed.

She covered her face with her hands, and turned her back to the lights. Seeping in from the sides of the room came the sounds of a mellow, sad saxophone evoking bittersweet thoughts of impossible love and velvet spaces beyond time.

She walked to the back of the room away from the lights to place her hands on the wall, to lean way in. The music rose and fell, her head swaying, keening with low rhythmic hums. Click. Click. Click.

She held her sides, turning around, bending at the waist to force herself up with an arched back with far flung arms to "Love for Sale," "Summertime," "I Loves You Porgy," and the theme from *Mondo Cane*. Click. Click. Click. Click. Click.

Her tears fell, steadily, her eyes mostly closed. The short black spandex skirt and the white man's sleeveless undershirt ala Calvin Klein lay close against her gently moving skin like loving hands. She caressed her sides and thighs with slow reassurance. Click.

"Bravo!" he shouted. "Bring up the house lights."

She looked up, her mascara running in double rivulets down her angular cheeks to spot her shirt. Her eyes rang wide, red-rimmed alarm.

"Babe," he said, gently, striding forward, his camera in one hand. "That's it! You were absolutely riveting. Wonderful!" Click.

He hugged her inexpressive form hard. Sound, hair, and make-up people, and of course, Barbara, walked briskly toward her to touch her face and hair, and to rub her shoulders.

"Wow!"

"A star!"

"I knew you could do it!" Click.

She began to shake.

"Wrap her in the velvet blanket, gang. Say, Ann, get

her one of the yellows in my top drawer to calm her down," he said.

"This is to New York," he squealed, planting a kiss on the camera.

Janitor

IN THE SEVENTH GRADE, in Sister Mary Viola's class, Beatrice Skowronski sat in the front seat near the front door. Stanley sat in the last seat near the last window along the outside wall. Beatrice, the youngest, slowest to mature girl in class, was small and delicate, with large blue eyes and wispy blonde hair. Everyone said she was pretty, which she was, but she was also sensitive and shy and modest. Stanley, one of the youngest of the boys, was tall and strong; but he was a kindred spirit to Beatrice—he was quiet, gentle.

Through six grades of school together, neither Beatrice nor Stanley paid particular attention to one another. Even in kindergarten and in the early primary grades when at recess the boys teased and chased the girls, Beatrice and Stanley played sedate games with small groups or stood on the periphery of activities, amusing themselves. Through the other grades and through fall and winter of grade seven, there was no change. Then spring came and abruptly, precipitated by the warming earth, Beatrice and Stanley were caught in the same field of sexual magnetism that affects all species.

Stanley began watching Beatrice; he sat up tall in his seat, stretched his neck to catch sight of her, and when there was recitation or blackboard work or recess or lunch or visits to the parish church for confession or mass, or when there was queuing up for dismissal, Stanley manuevered into positions to see her neck, her profile, a lock of her blonde hair, the feminine thinness of her youthful body. This went on for a time, seemed to Stanley sinful in its obsessiveness, but he couldn't stop. It was hopeless.

Then, as in a miracle, as in Czestochowa or Lourdes, Beatrice began turning to look at Stanley. She smiled, blushed, delicately touched her hand to her face and hair. She moved her seat back, just slightly, to see him, and so the two of them flirted shyly, not without a degree of youthful Catholic shame. It was agonizing yet blissful.

"Beatrice!"

Beatrice would turn quickly, feign having scratched her ear or the back of her neck. "Yes, Sister?"

"Rise, Beatrice."

"Yes, Sister."

Stanley's heart sank. Had she been caught?

"Help Mr. Olszowy with his spelling please."

"Yes, Sister."

It was just this: Now, because Beatrice stood, Stanley saw more of her—the roundness of her shoulders, her straight back, her narrow waist, her hips, her long sweet legs.

"Well, go ahead, Beatrice."

Oh, God, she didn't know the word!

"Proszem Wielebna Siostra, may I have a re-pronounciation?"

She is genius, Stanley thought. He smiled openly, felt he might have willed and transmitted this cleverness. He loved her, as God loves man. Stanley and

Beatrice were a single heart beating, a single mind thinking.

"Renounced," Sister said. "Re-noun-ced. As in 'Satan renounced his right to heaven for eternity.'"

"Renounced," Beatrice said, her voice joyous, "R-E-N-O-U-N-C-E-D. 'Satan renounced his leadership over the angels of the heavens.'"

"Thank you, Beatrice. You may sit."

Beatrice sat, and Stanley's heart pounded.

"So there, Chester Olszowy," Sister said, "as it's supposed to be spelled. Rise, give it another try. Be sure to pronounce the word, spell it, use it in a sentence. Ready now—"

For weeks, Stanley and Beatrice continued their flirtation, their two faces always shyly corpuscularly pink. Stanley loved the feminine facial aspects of Beatrice, her soft clear skin, her large eyes, her little ears; and Beatrice loved the masculine aspects of Stanley, his sharp features, his curly hair, the ruddiness of his complexion. Absent from their flirtation were actual speech between them and physical contact. Their love was innocent and genuine, a first love of purity and virtue.

Because Stanley sat in the back of the class, it was of course easier for him to flirt with Beatrice than for her to flirt with him. Stanley waited for Beatrice's turns, smiled or winked, either unabashedly open or disguised depending on Sister Mary Viola's degree of distraction. But Beatrice did not want to flirt any less then Stanley; it was a compulsion for her as it was for him. She dropped pencils, retrieved them, scratched her neck, adjusted barrettes in her hair, perpetually turned her necklace with the Sacred Heart of Jesus from back to front. Her smiles and glances were, thus, all the more appealing because they had about them the playful impishness and deceit of her confirmed admiration. Stanley loved her all the more.

It was inevitable. Sister Mary Viola was not a fool. For days she had been turning to the blackboard to write catechism, had been dropping her chalk over and over, each time stooping, looking back under her arm where her habit drooped.

Finally, one day, she stood and shouted, "Beatrice!"

Beatrice, in the midst of an open, intemperate smile, snapped her head to the front and rose. "Yes, Sister." She knew she had been caught.

Stanley too knew this, and aware of imminent confrontation, his lips quivered and the back of his neck grew cold. At first, his fear was personal; he was afraid that he too would be caught and reprimanded. Then, with his selfishness an embarrassment to him, he focused on Beatrice's dilemma, on her standing alone and culpable.

"I have been watching you, Beatrice," Sister Mary Viola said, "and last night in a vision the Virgin Mary, Mother of God, appeared and spoke to me. She told me what to do in your case."

Not just Stanley, rather the entire class listened intently. There was an atmosphere of suspense and terror. Everyone knew that Sister liked Beatrice, that though shy she was perceived to be the brightest and most spiritual. The students sat tall in their seats, stared reproachfully.

"Lustfulness is a boy's sin, Beatrice," Sister said, "not a girl's. Do you deny that you have committed a boy's sin?"

"No, Sister," Beatrice said honestly. There was a faint hint of moist contrition on her cheeks, wetness in her eyes.

"When boys commit sins, where do we send them?"

"Sister, we send them—"

"Not you, Beatrice. Stanley,—you tell me where we send them."

Stanley rose. His legs shook. The air in the class seemed thick and hot, almost unbreathable.

"Well, Stanley."

"Sis-ter," his voice broke, "we s-s-send them to the Judge."

"Chester Olszowy, where do we send the boys when they commit sins?"

Chester rose. "To the Judge, Sister."

"And Bernie Koczela. And Richard Koscielniak. And Walter Wnuk. And Matthew Bober. And Francis Michalenko. Where do we send them?"

They all stood. "To the Judge, Sister."

Stanley's knees felt shaky; he felt they would bend and he would collapse to the floor. He began to sit down.

"Stand, Stanley," Sister said, and so Stanley was made to stand as one of Beatrice's accusers. He looked at Beatrice, and just for a moment she looked at him. In both their eyes there was guilt and shame.

Then one by one, the entire class, first the rest of the boys then all the girls, rose on Sister's command. "To the Judge, Sister," they said in answer to her question. "To the Judge."

At the end, after hearing these onerous repetitions, Beatrice, overcome, slowly melted to the floor; her head fell like an unbearable weight into her hands, and she emitted deep, dolorous sobs from her heaving chest.

Then Stanley began to cry too, and though classmates looked at him quizzically, wondering why, Sister knew. "Such remorse is good for a boy," she said.

Just before recess, Beatrice was remanded to the Judge. She left the class to walk the length of the corridor to descend the dark service stairway to the dank basement and low, steamy boiler room. In a corner beneath a web of pipes, the Judge sat at his steel work desk, his bag lunch and thermos there, his coveralls draped over a chair, little pads of papers, stubs of pencils, keys and tools hung on the walls, wrenches, hammers, screwdrivers.

Outside it was bright, sunny, generously warm. At recess the children of the school spilled out into the schoolyard, and the grade seven students took to their area, Stanley among them but alone. Sister Viola was there too. She stood on the hill, her arms tucked into her dark habit, her eyes stern, looking down.

At the very bottom of the school building a little metal door opened. This was a scheduled opening; usually the Judge or a mischievous boy emerged. But this time, from the darkness of the school's basement, Beatrice emerged. She was thin and frail and feminine; a sunbeam caught in her sundress, sparkled. But then she turned, and the Judge set out of the door for her a large grey trash barrel. She tried to pull it, but it was circular and almost tipped. She tried to heft it (it spun and almost took her down in her first attempt), but then she succeeded, balancing it against her back, carrying it dolefully with her head down. As she moved slowly across the schoolyard to the large dumpster, students moved away from her disapprovingly, while Stanley, watching the Judge set out another trash barrel and another and another, did not move at all either to show disapproval or to help. Instead, he turned his gaze deliberately to willowy Maryanne Ordyna, began watching her long auburn hair blowing in the breeze, blowing and blowing, untarnished by the wages of a boy's sin. Meanwhile, Sister Mary Viola, seeing everything, closed her eyes in a quiet, blind affirmation of the catechism she had taught so well.

Janitor

*T*HE NOTE on the kitchen counter read: "Wer out and arond chacing janiter ha ha love Stuey." I set down the two bags of groceries I'd been squeezing to death, and peered out the kitchen windows which viewed our long driveway, and the cemetery just across the street. I didn't see any kids around; if I didn't hear from Stu soon, I'd take a walk up the street.

"Who's janitor?" I thought. "Janitor? Must be a dog." These early spring days found the neighborhood kids often down by the brook which scared me. The water whooshed along at a rapid pace. Kids could fall in. Stu knew that I didn't want him to hang out there. Still, I couldn't watch him every minute. "Damn," I thought. "It would be so nice to just sit and read awhile, but no."

The phone rang.

"Hi mom!" Stu's voice was giggly.

"Stuey, where are you?"

"At Rachel's."

"Where's that?"

Just then, I heard several children's voices whoop, and in the background, a sort of a wail, like from a younger child who'd broken a toy or something.

"Stu?"

There were muffled sounds from his end of the phone.

"Stuart, talk to me this instant!"

"Mom?"

"What?"

"Can we come over?"

"Who are we?"

"Everybody here, 'cept Janitor!" Again there were giggles, and the sounds of pushing.

"Stuart, listen to me. Where are you? I want you home, now!"

"Aw, Mom! C'mon, we're at Rachel's."

"Where is that?"

"Near Thorliebank."

"I'm going to ask you again—who is there with you?"

"Well, there's Rachel and Brian, Matt and Emily, me and Brooke, and . . . "

"Is Rachel's mother there?"

"Not yet." Just barely audible, he whispered aside from the phone, "There's trouble."

"I want you home now, non-negotiable. Five minutes, tops!" I hung up the phone feeling my stomach begin to tighten. Eleven year olds! Whatever happened to model airplanes, or kicking around a soccer ball? Have the times changed so desperately? Have I missed a transition?

I stood by the kitchen window watching the muddy flat of the driveway. Puddles and ruts made transit there bumpy and unstable—I'd have to see about getting some gravel dumped there; but there just never seemed to be enough time to do everything. Maybe even anything. Since my brother's funeral, I didn't have a lot of energy; I'd let a lot of things go, probably even the kids.

At the end of the driveway appeared a collage of color, reds, blues, pinks and yellows dancing in and around each other. The kids, mottled against the dreary day, moving energies along their collision courses, bumping squarely into me, grabbing my attention, catching me a bit off balance. They ran forward, then retreated, managing to hit the big puddles, laughing like crazy, totally unconcerned with consequences. Kids. Wonderful, scary beings. The boys were clearly showing off, leaping over and into the muddy places, dripping and red-faced from screaming and laughing. The girls followed, more gingerly through the gook, giggling, occasionally picking up some mud and slinging it at one of the moving boys. My stern position softened just watching them from my window—this last dance of their innocence was beautiful, something to remember for both of us when worry and temptation would become more intense.

I met the gang on the side porch, my presence before them almost a stunning blow. Their faces watched mine; their muddy wildness contrasted totally with my dry, prim appearance.

"Do your mothers know you are here?"

The kids looked at each other, but no one answered.

"Well, then. Is one of you Rachel?"

Stu pointed at a curly red-head in a hot pink, puffy parka.

"Rachel? Did you leave your mother a note?"

"No. She won't care."

"Well, I sure would." I stood there, not too sure what to do. I knew the boys well; the girls were just names, but I decided not to be hard-nosed. "O.K., then . . . "

Something light-colored moved in the bushes to the

left of the porch. Stu's eyes followed mine.

"Oh, gross!" he shouted. "Pox! Plague! Escape!"

"The janitor!!!" several voices shrieked in unison, the bodies taking off in two directions around the house.

"Janitor?" I said to the light spot in the bush.

Out of the underbrush a little human form wiggled, a pig-tailed, flame-haired little girl, maybe around five years old. Her oversized once white sweatshirt was stuffed into her bibbed jeans, one strap unfastened; her rubber boots were on the wrong feet.

"Janitor?" I said again.

She nodded, tear tracks streaking her face, her chest heaving.

"Are you with the kids?" I asked trying to understand what was going on.

She nodded.

"Well, then, come sit on the steps here with me a minute, O.K.?"

She moved cautiously over to sit on the bottom step.

"Stuart?" I called. "Come here this minute." Janitor startled. "It's O.K. honey," I soothed. "Hang on here a minute."

"God, Mom. I can't get close to her." Stuart said, keeping his distance from the porch.

"You'll come here, now!"

"What?" he whined.

"I want to know what's going on here. Who does this child belong to?"

"She's Rachel's brat sister."

"What's her name?"

"Janitor!"

"C'mon . . . "

"I don't know, mom. Just Janitor's all I know."

"Stu, you round up the kids, and go in the house—coats and boots in the basement. Then sit at the kitchen table. I'll be in soon."

"Aw, mom . . . "

"I mean it, Stuart."

The kids walked slowly up the porch steps past Janitor and me to disappear into the house. I walked down to the bottom step to sit next to the little waif—to offer her solace.

"Honey? Would you like a little ice cream?"

She looked at me with wide hazel eyes, and nodded solemnly. A large, insistent lump formed at the back of my throat.

"You know," I struggled, holding onto her grimy little hands. "My brother used to call me The Bird."

The Affair

THE HOUSE was just a little one, once a cabin possibly for deer hunters, or for someone like her, a city person who took rustic weekends in the country. But she had modified it for more pleasurable living. She knocked down interior walls, leaving attractive rough-hewn beams and larger, open spaces between kitchen and dining room and sun room. Then she opened exterior walls, inserting large glass windows and sliders and bringing in spectacular views of the Alford River Valley and the lilting rise and fall of the beautiful Berkshire Appalachians.

He was in the sun room, sitting on a white wicker chair. He had the Times puzzle and a pencil, but he wasn't thinking puzzle; he was staring out over the valley, thinking how he and his father used to take buses from Adams, their little grey mill town, carry along their fishing gear, hike miles from the center of Great Barrington to fish for trout in the Alford. Now, here he was, a poor man's son, blandly, dispassionately, overlooking the river he and his father had fished.

She was rich, of course, her father the owner of a giant Massachusetts construction firm. She was educated at Miss Hall's, at Wells, and at some school he never heard of in Switzerland. She was at the stove, dropping batter onto the grill, making Swedish pancakes. She was in a tan lambswool robe, looking attractive, her hair blonde and beautiful, fixed in New York for one hundred dollars a week. He liked a lot of things about her, her intelligence (she spoke seven languages), her strength and energy, her impeccable taste in clothes, her friendly eyes, her dimples, her light happy laugh like wind chimes. But she was short, about five foot one inch, had to do a lot of things on her toes, including dance with him, kiss him, take off his clothes. And, she was up on her toes now, as she often was though she didn't have to, dropping pancake batter onto the grill, piling up made pancakes, smiling, giggling. When he looked at her, he saw her tiny woman body, her tiny arms and hands and feet, visible out from the robe. She saw him looking, smiled broadly, blew him a kiss. He quickly turned, raised puzzle and pencil.

It was always like this with her kind of woman. They were all crazy about him, brazen in their pursuit of him, finding him in all kinds of places, red-neck bars, stream-side fishing, even in the woods during black powder season for deer. They knew him and of him, their noble savage, needing their care, their teaching, their play, their unrestrained lovemaking. But he knew them, too, knew their life was one of possession and greed. And he knew himself.

"They're coming," she sang out. "Can you smell the orange?"

"Huh?"

"And I have strawberries. I drove up early yesterday, picked fresh ones for you." Then she started singing, "La, la, la . . . tra, la, la . . . vita . . . vita . . . vita . . ."

Of all those he had known, she was the hardest. What was he going to do with her? She called him from the city at work and at home, leaving little bell noises on the answering machine that he bought specifically to keep her from calling, from flirting with the danger that his wife would answer, begin to ask, after so many calls: Who the hell is it? It's someone you're seeing, isn't it?

She got up on her toes, grabbed a pancake off her stack of made pancakes, tiptoed over to him. "Open up, agrements de la vie."

He tipped his head back, opened his mouth, but she dragged the pancake across his lips, over his nose. "Uh, uh," she said. She dropped the pancake into her robe, let it rest on her chest. "A la Francaise."

Games of possession, like the phone calls. It had finally and predictably evolved into this. He knew why they loved him, then hated him. His games were serious ones; then he got sick of theirs.

She shrugged her shoulders until the pancake slipped down. "Oooh."

"C'mere!" He reached out, grabbed her robe by its sash, pulled her down. She was so tiny, she dropped easily, like a child onto his lap. "What have you got there?"

"Nothing."

"Well, I know that."

"Bastard!"

He reached in under her robe, felt the warm little pancake resting on her tummy. She squirmed, but he held her down, moved the pancake in little circles.

"It's warm," she cooed. "It feels like a powder puff, mmm."

Her robe had ridden up; he looked at her little arms, her little legs, her tiny little thigh and calf muscles. He pushed the pancake down into her panties, against her little hair muff, patted it.

"Mmm, mmm, basso continuo."

Then he pushed the pancake against her, roughly, very roughly, until it broke, its battered pieces crumbling and falling, mushing up between his fingers, being smeared into, sticking to her hair.

"Oh, shit!" she kicked and tried to stop him, but he caught her little arms, held them. She raised her head, was looking for a kiss, for him to start that way, apologetically, then to take her roughly, as she liked him to. But he released her arms, raised her off his lap onto her feet, slapped her bottom.

"That bottom slapping's gratuitous, you know that." She went to the grill, removed a couple smokey pancakes, kicked open a little wastebasket, dropped them in. Then, up on her toes, she left for the bathroom.

He could hear the toilet flushing and water running in the sink. He imagined she was bent forward, picking out the pancake batter from her crotch, pulling and washing each pubic hair, one at a time. He imagined how small she must have looked doing this, as small as she was doing most everything.

It wasn't long, she came out of the bathroom, whistling, then singing, "Tra, la, la . . . vita . . .vita, vita . . ." She walked to the stove, got up on her tiptoes, dropped fresh batter onto the grill. He turned his attention to the Alford River Valley, his father, their fishing days together. He was in a reverie, deep, nostalgic, euphoric, when he realized she was on her tiptoes, upon him, ladling batter and smearing it into his hair.

"Affolé."

The Affair

I KNOCKED MY USUAL 'da da t'da-da', and it took him the usual while to answer his door. The glimmer of recognition. The smiles, the checking out past one another what was going on. The O.K. to come in. The sighs, and the watching for facial details: Signs of stress, longing, exhilaration, sadness, burdens, surprises beneath surfaces. Then comfort, and a blissful sense of calm. The acceptance and awe that this indeed was a real and important place to be. Before recently, we met in our cars at various lots. He's since left his wife and found this place to live where we have met, like this, and have etched our story into the furniture, onto the walls, and about the spaces mostly his. It's a place where we can be and have some privacy; sometimes a place to be, even alone. I have a key. Beyond the door, down a hallway, we met in the brightly lit kitchen. There was a table with two chairs, a heavy hotel ashtray midway between. There were dishes done, and a waste-can needed to be emptied. There were bills heaped on top of the refrigerator, a little one's pictures stuck there, and the 'whuzzz' of an electric motor to cool the food beast.

We hugged tightly. There was no past or future in the holding on. It was now as our hearts left impressions on the chests of each. Our smells merged to fuel the heady incense of need, lust, oneness, shared vision and wishful thinking. We made love there, using the wall for ballast, standing up only by the composite tenacity of our spirits. Our souls lost substance and form; incredible pleasure guided us over the minefield of our separateness until at last, filled and relieved, we met again on the kitchen floor.

"Can I take your coat?" he asked softly, still holding me close, catching his breath, his arm and neck muscles quivering.

"So soon?" I answered, smiling, still aware of his presence inside me, and my orgasmic aftershock. "Gee sus!"

"MMMMM," he agreed.

"Well," I sighed.

We pulled away from each other just enough to regain some natural balance, and composure.

"I love you. This," he nuzzled into my neck.

"Oh yes! You! This!" I whispered into his clean smelling hair, suddenly aware of potato chips fallen on the floor. "Messy, messy," I giggled.

"Oh God! Jamie's mess, one of many from this weekend." He ran his fingers through his hair, struggling to sit up. "Can I get you a drink?"

"Of course," I smiled, not wanting to let him go. "Oh well, I'll just use the john. Where shall I meet you?"

"In the big chair?"

"1040, my love!"

Sitting, facing him, straddling his lap, I clinked his glass to toast all that was good with us and the world. The Holidays were just past and there were days between then and now which seemed a void.

"Was it tough for you to get here?" he asked, stroking my eyebrows.

"A little, but . . . "

"But you're here. With me."

"Yes," I purred, kissing his eyes. "Did you have a nice Christmas?"

"Could've been worse. Sally didn't harp about Jamie's visiting me.; my folks were civil, and the rent's paid."

"That's nice. How about New Year's? Did you go out with George and his wife?"

"I think so," he teased. "If I can remember . . . "

"Oh please remember," I begged, nibbling his ear.

"Well," he began," George's wife was a little close all evening, if you know what I mean."

"I don't blame her," I said, moving my left leg over to cradle in his lap. "I hope you gave her the cold shoulder."

"I just found someone else to dance with."

"Oh, I see, you lady killer."

"Nah, actually it was George's brother-in-law's cousin that asked me to dance."

"Male or female?" I asked, stirring my drink with my finger.

"Does it really matter?" he asked back, running his finger down my right thigh.

"Of course it matters," I laughed, clutching his neck with my hands.

"I give," he yelped. "Her name was Cheryl."

I finished my drink and asked to have another. This time, I settled on the floor next to his legs as he sat in the chair. "So Cheryl kept George's wife at bay?"

"I guess she did!" he laughed.

I raised up on my knees, and leaned my arms forward onto his lap, watching his face. He proceeded to tell me about how Cheryl was recently divorced, living with relatives 'til she could make ends meet. She was a teller at the County Bank, and was studying accounting at night. His voice while he talked was upbeat, newsy. He gestured, smiled, told of his and Cheryl's clinking glasses for luck in the new year only to break glass and spill Jim Beam all over their fronts. So much for luck in the new year. He laughed. I watched his eyes, which saw the scene he was telling about as it happened. No wrinkles. A lightness. A silliness. A chance to let off steam and have fun in public. His lips, which a while ago had caressed my body so knowingly aware of my pleasure points, smiled now, easily framing healthy teeth in an open, boyish way. "I hadn't danced a polka in years!" he addead joyously. Part of me was Medea, scorned, filled with failed intentions and obsessed with what was not really mine. Part of me was mom, who wanted her boy to be happy in the proper scheme of things. Part of me wanted all of him, and was fit to kill interlopers. Part of me feared the borrowed time he and I had grabbed so hungrily beyond legitimate reason. His cheeks were rosy as he told of George's wife walking him into his apartment, here, and taking off his shoes and socks after he plopped down on his bed. Did he miss me? Did he and I have a future? I touched his cheeks and reached up to kiss his eyes. Did it matter what I thought? Did I love us more than him?

I settled back on the floor leaning against his legs. The fingers of his right hand played with my hair, his left hand held the cigarette he quietly smoked. The clock above our heads click-clocked.

"I'm glad," I said, my heart pounding hard, "that you had fun with your friends."

Asparagus

IT WAS EARLY spring and the fine little shoots of asparagus his grandmother had planted long ago poked their heads up through the grass. The asparagus was delicate, but it kept coming up year after year, insistently, though his mother ignored it, and his father had sodded over the old garden, tried his best to turn it into lawn.

But there they were— the little shoots; he could see their heads, grand and proud, poking through in a long straight row.

He recalled when his grandmother, her back bent over, dug one foot deep trenches, filled them half-full with chicken manure, made a mud of soil and water. He was very young, five or six.

" Co ty tam robisz, Babci?"

"Ah . . . widzisz!" she said, and this is all she said, because after her stroke one side of her face was non-expressive, and all but "widzisz"in her vocabulary was lost forever. "Widzisz" meant "to see," but it meant other things too: "to understand," "to perceive," "to witness," "to be embarrassed by," "to exult in," "to share with," "to see the result of, both of

---

Widzisz (Pronounced vee-geesh, Polish second person singular of widziec, to see.)

foolishness and of wisdom." His grandmother did not say "widzisz" to everyone. To his uncle and his father, she was silent; to his mother, it depended on circumstances; but to him, she said it all the time—"widzisz," "widzisz," "widzisz," moving the side of her face that could move, making expressive gestures with her hands.

For weeks he watched her while she made mud in the trenches, stirring the soil and water in with chicken manure. Finally, there was a powerful smell and floating green circles of mold. She brought finer soil in the wheelbarrow, an extra watering can, a trowel, and from the basement an old wicker basket filled with asparagus crowns.

She knelt down, deftly, gently separated the tangled roots. She placed a crown in the trench, took a trowel full of soil, let it sift in and around the crown. The crown poked up its head deep within the safety of the trench. She separated the roots of another crown, planted it a foot from the first.

"Widzisz," she said.

Then she gave him the trowel. She held the crown, and he dumped the soil in.

"Widzisz, widzisz!" she said. She took the trowel back and showed him how to spill the soil gently, not to dump it roughly. They planted together, her setting crowns in, his spilling the dirt, gently, until they had filled an entire trench. She pulled him to her then, his little child's body to her bosomy chest; she hugged him, and he hugged her back. "Oh . . . oh . . . widzisz!" she said, and she smiled from the one side of her face.

For many days in a row, he and his grandmother tended the trenches, adding soil, and watering. Each time the little asparagus tips poked through, they covered them. Gently. Together.

Then fall came, and winter; and the following spring when the asparagus came up, it was admired but not harvested. Then another year went by, and his grandmother had another stroke. This time her left eye closed up completely and her right hand shriveled. But when spring came, and the asparagus came up, she sharpened a knife, using one hand and an elbow pressed against her side, and so went out and cut asparagus spears.

She made kapusta with both prawdziwe and zólty mushrooms; she made potato pancakes, and kielbasa, and borszcz, and hard-boiled eggs, and blueberry pierogi, and steamed asparagus spears made over the boiling pierogi. She snapped the spears, and they broke perfectly where they were tender. She set the food on his plate and covered the asparagus with Bearnaise sauce.

"Widzisz!" she said.

He ate pleasurably and she watched him. He loved the asparagus, ate seconds without sauce, with just butter and lemon.

And now here were the tips busting through the sod of his father's lawn, from the old garden and the old trenches, ignored by his mother. He knelt down, looked closely at the asparagus. They were so perfectly aligned, even after all these years. For a moment he saw his grandmother ahead of him, her back bent, placing crowns. He was following with his trowel and dirt. He hadn't realized at first, but he had scraped up a hunk of sod with his fingernails, the dirt digging into his skin making him bleed. In that little spot, he thought he could see the trench, the outline of the trench. He looked ahead and smiled.

"Widzisz," he said to her, "widzisz!"

Asparagus

*H*E CALLED at my office to ask me out for dinner. He knew a cute little French restaurant in a neighboring town.

"You? A French restaurant?" I asked, amazed. "You who won't even eat my . . . "

"Pam," he said, "Pam, trust me. I have my reasons, you'll see."

He waited.

"I'll have to see to the kids."

"Please," he said in his best, deep soft voice. "Let me take care of it."

"Yes?"

"Yes."

"You'll pick me up here after work then?"

"Yes."

Oh my God! This was excellent! I ambled, smiling, into the john to check myself out. Hair sort of stringy. Face, wan. I could rev it up? Sure. Some hairspray here, some blush there, some nail polish, some mouthwash, and a squirt or two of scent should do the trick. Definitely I would pull myself together. No rush home on the T line. No leftover meatloaf. No evening of T.V. re-runs and the incredible, everlasting summer stamina of two young boys. Tonight, Tuesday, would be just George and me at a romantic French restaurant. George at a romantic French restaurant? Good God! The man was a baseball and hotdog freak. Hamburgers and steak were his meats of choice. Mashed potatoes with rolls rounded things out. Sometimes a raw carrot. Huh?

I wet a paper towel to press against my forehead and cheeks. I tried to imagine George walking into someplace other than HoJo's or Beafsteak Charlie's. Yet somehow, I could see it. He had great manners. He ate neatly, slowly, never changing his silverware nor talking with his mouth overloaded. He hadn't traveled much, or so he said; but he was fastidious with dining details like doing the ordering for us both, even if it were spaghetti, and laying his napkin, paper or cloth, quietly across his knee. While the dinner could be declassé, dining with George was always sacred.

O.K. O.K. Enough about George and food. It would be interesting, period. I was, after all, just finding out about him. We'd met playing golf; he had his son on weekends when my ex had my boys. Even though we hadn't spent a great deal of time together, I could feel a slowly slung net of affection catching us up and pulling us closer. We had only kissed a couple of times and I wondered if he wanted to touch me.

Bosh! I tossed the paper towel into the basket. I'd keep my head this time. I'd stay cool. I knew I'd love French food, even escargots. We could each certainly take care of ourselves.

By the time the asparagus arrived at the La Foliage, I felt both warm and lightheaded. Good Lord! Two and a half bottles of wine, gonezo! George ordered flawlessly in French, translating for me the choices of sauces and herbs. We had just finished artichoke hearts in vinaigrette, when the maître d' gracefully slid between us an oval plate full of slender, firm asparagus with delicate heads, garnished with star shaped truffles, dusted with purple basil, and accompanied by a small tureen of melted butter.

"Mmmmmmm," hummed George, taking my hand and kissing its palm. "This is why I come here. These asparagus are the specialty of the house." He inhaled deeply, his eyes closed, and gave me back my hand.

The maître d' smiled and bowed. More wine was poured as I sat transfixed.

"George, this is incredible!" I shuddered to think about the cans or the frozen wads of asparagus chunks I tried to serve my kids sometimes. Obviously, I had missed the ceremony, the high etiquette of this strange smelling vegetable. Unlike the George I'd previously witnessed, I ate anything green; but now, I felt more awed than hungry— excited, really, to observe his next move.

His thick fingers daintily lifted an asparagus shaft, to dip its tip into the butter. He extended it toward me, and I reached up to take it from him.

"No, no," he cautioned. "Please, just suck it gently. Let the flavor tease your tongue. That's right, go ahead."

I steadied his hand with both of mine, and I felt the head enter my mouth, which watered almost to the point of drooling. I closed my eyes sensing the knobby green more than tasting it beneath the salty butter.

"Don't bite," he whispered. He eased the vegetable back out of my mouth. "That's right, darling."

My head was swimming, my hands still touched his. Oh my God! Oh my God!

"Jesus, George, I . . . "

"Shh. Watch me."

Guiding one of my hands with his, he worked his lips over the asparagus head, working his mouth back and forth until the tip pulled loose.

"Mmmmmmm, this is so good." He chewed a little, swallowed, and squeezed my hand. "Your turn," he said, his eyes direct into mine.

I reached for my wine to take a sip, holding his gaze, dribbling some down my chin into my lap. Still, we watched each other. My hand was a little shaky yet I managed to extend an asparagus tip dipped in butter to him. His lips were full and soft upon the head, moving just a little to and fro with suction. Next, I pressed my lips down hard against the tip to make it my own. It was succulent, deliciously fresh.

My toes found his legs under the table, and with one hand, he reached down to massage them. We continued to enjoy the asparagus, my desire for him growing more urgent than for the vegetable between us.

"George . . . "

"Yes?" he whispered.

"I'm full now."

"But there's more," he said, stroking my calf.

Fat

THEY WERE VACATIONING in Canada, in gloriously beautiful Vieux-Quebec, the Old City. This evening they were dining out at the Cafe de la Paix. They arrived early, so the maître d' gave them a choice little table for two near an open window where they could hear street sounds and watch people passing by.

They had already ordered the table d'hôte, had finished a marvelous bisque which their waiter had dismissed as "jus' ve-gét-able soup," and were now into their salad with vinaigrette.

"Have you noticed," she said, "that the servings are all small? Yet I've felt full wherever we've eaten."

"French cooking. You were in Paris. Wasn't it the same?"

"Yes, very much."

"And isn't this salad typical? A few lettuce leaves, some oil, and it's delicious."

She chewed on some salad, smacked her lips, nodded in agreement, then she said, "Wasn't he funny, our waiter, 'Jus' ve-gét-able soup'? I mean, *just!* It was wonderful. Oops, I'm out of water."

A busboy appeared, poured a refill. "Madame!"

"Merci."

When the busboy left, she leaned over the table. "Do you think they read minds?"

"Just good service."

"That's right, *just!*"   She took a sip of her water. "I mean, how many waiters do we have? And look at them, they're all thin and handsome. That one, with the curly hair, he's the best looking."

"What amazes me is how they can work around food like this and stay so thin."

Outside, at the restaurant entrance, the maître d' was responding to two couples, New Yorkers or from Jersey.

"Yez, ala carte or complet dinérs, however you wish it is, but we are all full up for zis evening. You wish tomorrow maybe?"

The men were fat, the women fatter. One of the men, balding, his belly drooping over his belt, spoke to the maitre d'. "Well, we've got to eat now, you see. Why would we want to wait twenty-four hours between meals?"

"That's it, Carl," his wife said. She was fatter than her husband, her knees joweled, fat ankles stovepiped into her high heels. "That's it, tell him, Jesus, he's got to find us a table. Tell him we've come a long way to eat his food. Tell him that."

The other lady, tall with large arms and a big chest, she spoke up: "I told you Marie. This afternoon I said we should make reservations. I said we should make a call, but, remember, I want you to remember, you said we should just show up."

This lady's husband had taken his sports coat off, was sweating through his white shirt. "That's right, Marie, we were going to call. We said we should call."

"Jesus," Marie said,"don't get your noses all out of joint. Carl's meat and potatoes is gate crashing. Isn't it hon? Isn't it your meat and potatoes?"

Carl turned his head from the maître d'. "Hey, don't worry, this guy here, he's like melted butter. I eat guys like him for lunch, don't I, Marie? Remember that guy in Mario's; now he was tough, but with just a little grease on the skillet— Open Sesame!"

Inside, at their table near the window, they could hear the couples talking, to one another, to the maître d'.

"Americans are stupid, aren't they?" she said. Sometimes I'm embarrassed for us, we're so overbearing."

"We're not."

"In general. I mean, the difference is staggering. Since we've been here I've developed a great respect for the French-Canadians. Every morning it's 'bon jour;' each evening it's 'bon soir;' and then it's 'merci' for everything. Jesus, you can eat off the sidewalks it's so clean."

"When I was jogging yesterday morning over there in the park, in the Plains of Abraham, all the Canadian joggers said hello, you know, 'bon jour;' the Americans turned their heads, or grunted."

"How could you tell who was who? Really, hon."

"You can tell, the Americans don't dress right. You know how we've seen the difference, the Canadians all loose fitting and comfortable. And they smile. Even if it was Americans saying 'bon jour,' they wouldn't be smiling."

"There they go again, outside."

"They're obnoxious."

Outside, Carl had stepped forward, slapped a bill into the maître d's hand.

"Monsieur, this is not necessary." The maître d' tried to give the money back.

Carl turned and smiled at his wife and friends, then turned back to the maître d'. "No you keep it. Use it on the skillet. You know."

"I insist, monsieur."

Carl pulled out another bill, also slapped this into the maître d's hand. "I insist too."

The maître d' was making an honest attempt to give the money back. He grabbed Carl's wrist, was trying to put the money into his hand.

"Keep it." Carl said. "I mean, it's yours, for the luvva. It's yours."

The maître d' composed himself, put the money into his pants pocket. "Merci."

For a while there was no conversation, nothing. The couples just stood there. The maître d' was motionless, his menu under his arm.

"Well," Carl said, "we're ready. Aren't we ready, Marie?"

He turned to his friends. "What do you say a few drinks in the lounge to whet our appetites?"

"On me, Carl. It's on me buddy." the other man said.

"So then, let's go there, Frenchie." Carl stepped forward, slapped the maître d' on the shoulder.

"I'm sorry, monsieur. Tonight the tables are full up, complet."

"Sure, okay pal, we gotcha." Carl winked. "Now show us to the lounge, it's hot out here."

"I'm sorry, c'est à dire, all tables have been reservér."

"Jesus, you're serious, aren't you, pal," Carl said.

"Complet aujourd'hui."

Carl wrinkled his lips, glared at the maître d'. He put one hand on his hip, stuck the other out forcefully.

The maître d' calmly reached back into his pants'

pocket, handed Carl the money he had been given.

"Now what, Carl?" the other lady asked.

"Stay cool, Muriel," Marie said. "Come on, Carl, let's go someplace where they're more friendly, where thy care about the impression they make on Americans, where they're not snotty and too good for everybody."

"Frenchie, you're a jerk, you know that," Carl said.

"Come on, Carl," Marie said.

"Merci," the maître d' said calmly.

"Mercy! Mercy? For the luvva— these Frenchies just lay down and roll over!"

The maître d' was composed, unperturbed.

Inside, they had finished their salads, their plates had been cleared. They could see outside that Carl and his wife and friends had moved closer to their window; they were whispering to each other, then began moving away.

"You're a jerk, Frenchie," Carl said, "a real jerk, you know that."

"Carl, let him be, the hell with him," Marie said.

Then they turned, began walking down the street, and from inside they could see them, the men broad and fat and sweaty, the women with the backs of their knees showing fat, ugly back of knee fat.

When Carl and the rest disappeared, the waiter came with their main course, frog legs for her, quail for him, with légumes du jour et pommes de terre, french beans and scalloped potatoes, and with little colored vegetable decorations, flowers and leaves.

"Look how small."

"Taste it."

She lifted a leg, took a nibble. "Oh, God, try it!

Here."

She held it out for him, and he took a bite; then he held out a piece of quail breast for her.

"Hmmm," she said, "these people know how to live."

"And stay thin."

"And remember?"

"What's that?"

"And stay handsome."

The handsome curly-haired waiter came to their table.

"Everything is tres bon?" he asked.

They indicated, "Mmm, yes. Yes it was, indeed."

Outside, the maître d' stood inscrutably, a twinkle in his eye, a slight smile on his face. He was waiting patiently for diners with reservations.

Fat

*T*WO FLAT-BELLIED, perfectly permed, painted-nailed, bikini-clad young girls stood calf deep in the lake facing the sun, maximizing their crowd appeal.

"Bimbettes," Zack called them.

"But damned cute," I said, sucking in my stomach.

"I think they'd agree with you," he joked, taking a slow drag on his cigarrette, squinting in the direction of the girls through his exhaled smoke.

"I'm gonna try not to feel jealous," I said, following his look. Yet inside I felt a threat. It had been a few years since I'd looked O.K. in a swimsuit. Usually now I tried to sit in the shade to avoid large freckles and dried out hair. After two kids, my belly was a soft round bump.

"See, what you don't see, dear, is that these girls look wonderful, but they are no fun!" he said.

"But if they're truly bimbettes, they'll come through later."

"Yea? Only if the male wouldn't muss or fondle with sweaty palms. And, God those nails wreak havoc," he grimaced.

"Then why, my love, do males seem to go gaga over these bimbs and kick sand in the faces of the girls who'd kill to be noticed?"

"I notice you!"

"Mmm, I'm real glad you do. Now."

"Hey, guys learn, some faster than others. They'll all eventually catch on," he reassured.

Just then a powerful cold water splash drenched us. "Geesus! What the . . . " I startled, straightened up and searched for the culprit. But as soon as I saw the splash source, I felt massively tickled. Jumping about in the water just beyond us were a pair of large girls, one dressed in cut offs and a tent- sized Van Halen tee shirt, the other in a mega black swim dress, the skirt of which was plastered up against her humungous thighs.

"Summer whales," Zack observed, toweling off and reaching to light another cigarette.

"Big Mamas! Whoa! Fat doesn't quite cover it," I added.

"But," he added seriously, "they ARE having fun, yes?"

"Spreading the cheer, too," I agreed, mopping off my face.

The bimbettes turned their backs to us and the sun, moving slowly so as not to make a ripple. Their small, tightly rounded bottoms set safely within bikini confines, no sags, no drags. Directly in front of them were three tanned, athletic lads in Ocean Pacific jams, tossing a frisbee, going for leaping saves to land and roll in the grass. They whooped and set up pass plays, failing to evoke more than a one-fingered wave from one of the lovelies.

Just then, the frisbee went wild with a hook into the water just beyond us. One of the whales squealed; "It's mine now, darlin'," as she dove her full weight against the blue plastic saucer.

"Toss it back," one of the boys shouted, hands on his hips.

"Come and get it," the big girls unisoned.

"Ah, gee — C'mon toss it!"

But the water babes just giggled, pushing their maxi shapes out toward the swim line limit.

"Shit," said the boy. He ran into the water diving at knee-high depth. One of the bimbs looked over her shoulder at the action, but turned around, unimpressed. The boy gained on the whales to dive at his frisbee. But the Van Halen gal was too quick, tossing it to her friend.

"Hey," he sputtered, surfacing. "It's mine, give it!"

"Pretty please with sugar on it," the other gal teased.

"Fuck this," he said, lunging at them. The three of them splashing each other, moving sizeable waves of water around, enough so to evoke a whistle warning from the guard.

"Help," he yelped, laughing as one of the whales dislodged his stance with a hip bump.

The other two boys heard their buddy and raced to the rescue, keeping a wide berth around the bimbs. Soon the frisbee was recaptured, but the game continued including the whales. Everyone who watched the waterplay smiled. It was a beauty—all laughs, splashes, and spectacular dives. At last they slowed down, gulping for breath, with high fives all around signaling the game's end.

"Don't y'all drown, now," the first boy said.

"We float good," giggled one of the whales.

As the boys eased themselves into shore, one of them splashed the bimbs.

"Asshole," one of the cuties said, walking back to her towel.

"It's the fat girls who always have fun," Zack said. "They have nothing to lose."

"They could lose a little, here and there," I observed.

"Well, he said, "think about it. It's summer, it's hot, and life goes on. These big gals will be chock full of memories. To the bimbettes, today is just another day like all the others wrapped tight around themselves."

"You're right, of course. Still . . . "

"Still what?" he asked, turning his full, loving, blue-eyed attention on me.

"Well, back a few years, I was too thin, too shy, and too victimized by razor rash to enjoy myself."

"It's never too late for a hot fudge sundae," he suggested.

Crazy

IT WAS LATE AFTERNOON. He had left his desk and typewriter, was sitting on the living room sofa. On his lap he had *The New Yorker* opened to a short story, and on an end table near him he had the daily crossword, begun but not finished, a pen, a pencil, a glass of generic soda water, half a ham sandwich, chips on the side. He had begun with the crossword but felt guilty this wasn't work; he raided the kitchen, began a snack, then part-way through switched the content of his nourishment. But now he wasn't reading or doing anything; he was just staring into space.

Catatonia— this was just one stage of his craziness. Other stages were dyslexia, arthritis, and death attacks, in this latter case anxiety so serious that he went beyond sweat, palpitations, and diarrhea all the way to brain splitting, wherein one part of his brain went out of his body, floated above him, looked down and commanded his death.

"Damn this fucking sofa!" This was one way of snapping out of things—disassociation. But then he noticed the television; it commanded his attention because it was broken, hit by a bolt of lightning once again, as if this sort of happening was common in artists' houses. And then he noticed the rest of the furniture, mixed and matched and old, and the lamps ugly, and the walls needing paint, and all other material objects within eyeshot old and worn and emblematic of the pain and strife and asceticism forced on him by his choice of career.

"God!" He thought of his wife, happy and cheerful, full of positive expectations. Didn't she know, he was a bad risk? The thought of her did him in, big eyes, wide smile, wondrous lady. She deserved better.

There it was! There was muscle pain on both sides of his elbows. His arms twitched, and soon, if he let things take hold of him, his hands would be sore and his fingers too clubby to type.

He hurried to his desk and typewriter. There was this morning's work, less than half a page:

> *He knew part of corporate strategy with waste was to release it into rivers and lakes and oceans and into the air, to hide killer refuse among life-giving molecules. His lungs, animal lungs, fish gills, all breathing apparatuses were constricted by General Electric's emissions of p.c.b.'s, toluene, dioxin. Toxins rode the airways, found a respiratory system, played havoc with red blood cells . . .*

This was truth, worth saying; but it was short story junk, polemical, not narrative. This bothered him deeply. Years ago he had gone past the pseudo-professorial stage in his writing. He wasn't telling, posturing, writing to academic formula and acceptability anymore; he was a singular mind, a singular soul, a one-of-a-kind writer. And now this. Crap!

He ripped the paper out of the typewriter, tried to replace it with another but ripped an edge rolling it in.

"Shit!" He threw the paper on the floor. His hands hurt; the arthritis, his fingers were so sore.

He looked at the clock. It was six already. His wife would be home from work soon. He looked at the paper on the floor, looked at the typewriter. From eight in the morning until six, there was nothing. Not a single page. There was catatonia, and pain in his muscles, and clubby hands and fingers. If he let things happen, there would be sweating, stomach cramps, diarrhea, then, at night when his wife slept soundly, his brain would split, one half drifting over the bed behind him, making its hellish demands on the other half.

He reached into his paper drawer, put another paper into the typewriter. He skipped all the titling and pagination. He struck some keys; they stuck. He unstuck them violently, then typed.

> *Frankie pedalled his ten-speed through the Coltsville intersection out toward Plastics Avenue and General Electric's new Plastics Technology World Headquarters Building. He was dressed in bicycling shorts, helmet, goggles, gloves, prepared for a fast approach and a fast get-a-way . . .*

Oh, God, this was worse than before! "Fast get-a-way : " this was crap out of a cheap thriller. One thing the university writers knew: they knew what was moribund. He hit the space bar, hit it, hit it. He smashed the goddam thing.

"Oh, my, little Frankie not writing good?" This was his wife, Barbara; he had not heard her come in.

"I didn't hear you come in."

"You were smashing the typewriter."

"Sorry."

"Smash if you want to smash."

"It's because I didn't get a word all day. Not a word."

"I didn't get anything either. I tried, but all the male customers were either married and faithful or going back to work and not in the mood for a quickie." She was always light about his writing, not that she didn't value it, she did; but her approach to his problems with it was always to gloss over trouble, as though that way the smoothness he needed to make things work would follow.

"Barbara, I'm serious."

"My crotch is itchy."

"I'm going to be sick. No shit."

She leaned over him, let her hair fall over him, gave him soft, palliative kisses on the back of his neck.

"Barbara, really, I got nothing."

She reached down, gently put her hand in his pants."Well, I know, but it's all right. After all this time I've learned to adjust."

"Oh, Jesus, Barbara, can't you be serious?"

"I am."

"I'm talking about writing."

"Let's talk about sex instead."

"Now?"

"You are a hard case. No, not now, let me get my calendar. Of course now. Oh, wait a minute." She reached further into his pants, her soft hand touching him there, her fingers feeling the parts of him. "Speaking of hard!"

"No it's not."

"But it's getting there. It wants to, I can tell. Get

down."

"What?"

"Get down." She was pushing him out of his chair onto the floor.

"Jesus!"

She was pulling up her skirt, removing her panties, getting ready to get on top of him.

"Mmmm. Mmmm. You poor crazy bastard," she was saying.

"Crazy?" But of course he knew this better than she. Because of her, he would have a peaceful evening, but then there was tomorrow, when without her the pain would come back, the sweating and the diarrhea, and the brain splitting. But he knew too, that after one week of craziness, his writing would all come back, smoothly, and the pain and anxiety would stop, and he'd get things right and be well again. But what about her? Talk about crazy—she'd never be well. No matter what happened to him, she believed in him. It was a chronic condition, unrelenting.

"Mmmm. Mmmm."

Crazy

THE NIGHT was as hot as steamed mustard greens; the warm air mixing with the dew made the darkness heavy with a fresh, green smelling fog. The day had been in the 90's; the sun's setting had not brought much relief, unusual for the Northeast. It was summer like I'd always remembered it in Indiana with fireflies and my running around in my underwear in the wet grass trying to cool off. Then, I was a little girl; now I was trying like hell to be a writer, but the words were stuck, hot and tired.

It didn't help that during the day I'd had to change both the correctotype and the typewriter ribbon twice trying to meet a deadline for a book of short stories I was finishing. Two stories to go. When the power went around eleven P.M., I had to call a truce. My husband picked his way cautiously down the basement stairs to check on the fuses; but this blackout was beyond us. The whole street was dark.

"Oh shit!" I said quite loudly.

"Why don't you come to bed. Even art has to rest," he added with a sly grin.

"Does this feel like the great seduction?" I countered.

"Flagellate yourself, see if I care." He handed me the flashlight and nodded toward the hutch." Candles in there; matches on the stove. Be a fool!"

"Be a jerk," I said feeling impotent in the face of this natural disaster.

I walked to the back door and shouted the F word two or three times into the soft night. So what if my fiddleheads might droop or my neighbors be once again disappointed at my lack of verbal control. "F them!!!" I thought, wickedly.

I wanted to write a story about my mother. She was dead now, but when she was alive, she was a pistol most usually aimed at me. But God damn! She was vivid soul. So why the hell was I so blocked? I had started out O.K.:

> "She grabbed my hand in the department store and hissed in my ear that I had better straighten up or I couldn't accompany her to the eighth floor tearoom for tea and those rolly-polly sandwiches.
>
> 'Mommy, my head hurts from the lights.'
>
> She just tightened her grip on my hand and led me to the elevator . . . ."

Then what? Reality seemed a blur and my imagination was somehow too mild for the indelible impression left with me that day, long ago, in the clutches of my mother.

I had also wanted for some time to write a story about sailing; partly, I wanted to please my husband who fretted that I didn't seem to enjoy our boat. My father had loved the whole aura of sailing, so I figured that I could somehow dredge up something like a commemoration, even if it were brandished. Water,

wind, flaps, gulls, and ropes were active, time-tested
images:

> "The wind pulled us along at a faster than
> usual pace. The water around us grew more
> turbulent and dark like a black stallion's mane
> at full gallop.
> 'Should we head in?' I shouted above the
> wind.
> 'Hell, no! This is great! No engine—it's all in
> the ropes.'
> 'Yes, but . . . ' A splash of cold water from the
> murky lake hit me hard between the eyes. I
> coughed.
> Suddenly the boat lurched over on its side,
> the wind changing direction petulantly, menac-
> ingly.
> 'Go lower the mainsail,' he ordered, stagger-
> ing for balance by the rudder.
> Dark clouds were rolling overhead and I was
> frightened. How could I stand up, somehow let
> go of the fickle jib lines, and crawl out over the
> cabin to locate the mainsail lines? The boat was
> now heeling at about 45 degrees; I looked up,
> and saw the mast begin a slow fall toward me,
> having sprung one of its pins . . . . "

Then what? Again, a blank. Too personal? What I
remember most was our five year old huddled in the
cabin, crying. Obviously we had made it back. But the
whys and wherefores were stuck.

I poured myself a third glass of good scotch. There
were no lights and there was no whirr from the fan. I

walked outside to sit on the back steps, and listen to the crickets and some toads rustling in the bushes. It was as hot as I had ever remembered in Indiana. The damp of the dew was even warm to my touch. The scotch made a loving furrow down in my esophagus, hot but friendly.

"MMMMM." I breathed deeply. Chives, thyme, dill, mint, and basil were close by. Not too far away were the lillies, iris, and phlox. Just beyond our yard lay my neighbor's vegetable garden, always prolific, always over-abundant, a reason I had given up my attempts to cultivate the same. I did a whole lot better with spices. So we exchanged.

I figured that too many air-conditioners and fans along with all other electric things had contributed to the blackout; from where I sat, it was going to be a long, dark, steamy night. I stood and stretched, re-membering what it was like when I was little, to take most of my clothes off and roll around in the grass to cool off. This time, I took everything off. I walked past my clothesline to hug one of the trunks in the birch tree clump. The bark felt rough against my skin. Some-where inside, between my heart and my skin, a glow-ing sensation started. This is what I needed. Basics. Feelings, not contrived thoughts on paper. I turned my back against the tree and eased myself down into a sitting position. Lights from passing cars beyond my yard were yellow speckles to drip from the branches overhead, and bushes nearby. The wet grass tickled the backs of my legs and up into my crotch. I reached down to press the grass and the wetness closer be-tween my legs; the blades became light, probing fin-gertips arousing my pleasure.

I shivered. I'd go into my husband. I'd wake him. Art needed stimulation before it could rest.

He'd responded, but in his half sleep, he'd come and gone rather quickly. As fast as he had roused, he was again, with little sweat, dead weight.

I thought that maybe I should go take a cool bath, but as unsatisfied as I was, I didn't want to lose the electric feelings, the needing female flesh, I possessed. Wasn't this the point? I needed to express myself. I needed to be able to gush out my feelings, perhaps the feelings of others like me —lonely and unfinished: Art as goad to self discovery.

My body wanted to suck something in, to hold it close, then let it go in a blaze of expression.

I wrapped myself in a towel and walked back outside to sit. The things I'd left earlier were still there, the wet grass, the passing lights, and the insect sounds. I wanted to let go.

Hugging and rocking myself there, I visualized a slow, deep release, while a neighbor's cucumber lengthened in the hot, dark dampness.

Male Child

My son, Aaron, and I are twenty years in the past. I am twenty-five, he is almost four. We sit on the bank of the Iowa River in Iowa City, both of us tanned as darkly as farmers. Two fishing rods rest against freshly cut saplings; long hooks are baited with river shad, the little fish dangling on the bottom, their tails wiggling in the current. The poles sag and release; the lines belly into the current.

I am alert, for a great tug or a sharp series of tugs which signal a blue cat. Aaron, typically child-like, is happy just to be with his father. He has brought his small suitcase of matchbox cars and trucks, has made miniature roads for them on the river bank.

"Drive over my house, okay Dad, then the two of us will visit old dziadziu."

I grab my car (the dear child has given me a Mercedes), begin moving along his roads toward where his car is parked.

"Your car's broke," he says. "I don't hear the engine."

So we "tow" the car to "Aaron's Garage" where he flips the car over, bites his lip, and with a twist of his little arm, repairs the car.

"It's fixed, listen."

He blows air into his closed lips. "Vroom, vroom."

"Hey, all right, good job there. You're quite a little mechanic."

"Big!"

"Uh?"

"I am a big mick-al-nic."

"Oh, yes, that's right," I say convincingly, "you are a *big* mechanic."

A smile lights his face.

I am about to drive my car, the Mercedes, over to his house. So I start the car.

"Vroom," he reminds me.

"Vroom," I say, "vroom, vroom," and the car runs in a low rich hum down the street, "rrrrroooom."

As I'm driving, a young couple, strolling along the riverbank, come up on us. I quickly turn my car around, with nary a sound from the engine, head back home.

"Hey," Aaron says, "wrong way."

"Guess what?"

"What's it, Dad?"

"I forgot . . . breakfast. I haven't eaten breakfast yet. Have you? I mean after your early morning work on my car at your garage, you're going to need some breakfast too."

The young couple is standing above us now, casting shadows on our world. I slip my hand off the car, reach over, adjust one of the fish poles.

"Any fish?" the young man asks.

"No, nothing yet."

"Been 'ere long?"

I turn to my son. "What do you say, Aaron, about a half hour?" Aaron does not tell time yet, nor does he understand, or for that matter accept, the concept. Phrases like "be back soon," or "in a while," or "about a half hour" threaten his little mind with the possible absence of those he loves and depends on. Yet, because I have been spending so much time with him, I have begun to include him in my conversations with other adults— occasionally, as in this case, turning to him to confirm my statements. Being with him, being apart from adult companionship for so many hours in the day, I have developed the quirks of a lonely housewife; my reliance on my child, just past infancy, is the most obvious of these quirks. Of course, on the positive side, doing this confirms our connectedness; and, sometimes, obliquely, I actually find myself looking to him for support.

" 'Bout a half hour," Aaron says, shaking his head as though he has thought about it, understood it temporally.

"Maybe a bit more or less," I say. "But we're fishing for blues, got lots of time."

"Hey, good luck to ya," the young man says. He has been interested in us, amiable—so I see now—because he has wanted to display his openness to experience in front of his girl; and—I see this too—he has wanted to show off his girl. She has red hair, green eyes, beautifully tanned skin for a red head; she has the fresh, healthy look of so many mid-western farm girls. She is attractive, unarguably. I look up at her, smile. The young man is proud. He steps back from us, puts his arm around his girl as though she has just arrived from a distant place.

They begin moving off, and the girl turns to Aaron. "Keep those cars running, garage-man." They each give friendly waves goodbye.

When I look at Aaron, he is beaming. A stranger has

called him "garage-man," thus reaffirming his image of himself in our little world.

I take my car in my hand, start it loudly. "Vroom, vroom!" The couple turns and smiles. Before I move the car, however, Aaron shouts at me, "Hey, Dad, you forgot to eat breakfast!"

Male Child

IT WAS SEVEN YEARS AGO that my son, then ten, announced that he wanted to dance in the Berkshire Ballet's annual *Nutcracker*. Although I considered myself a sexually unbiased parent, giving Phip dolls as well as cars and trains along the way, I was a bit shaken by this large-for-his-age sports ace wanting to dance. Well not dance exactly, but do ballet. I mean, I had taken years of ballet as a kid, and had never seen a boy. I loved watching professional ballets, and of course there were men dancing. But never lots. I t seemed that for every luscious Baryshnikov or Nureyev there were a sissy or three. But it was Phip's decision, and he appeared quite sure.

The audition for parts was what I imagined it would be like on Broadway: There was an upright piano in the corner of a large, wood-floored, and big-windowed room with tall, exposed radiators; a thin, chain-smoking older man sat at the piano obeying without expression the shrill commands of the ballet mistress; and everywhere there were stretching, scurrying, and anxious folk of just about every age group. Phip, normally independent and uninvolved with me, stayed close by my side. The children were mostly little girls dressed in their dance class pink or black leotards, pink tights, and pink, well-worn dance slippers. I counted five boys, other than Phip, all in jeans and tee shirts sporting logos from soccer camps, or *Kiss,* or "Suzuki Does It Better." Phip, who usually wore whatever was on the top of any drawer, took special care that day: He wore bleached(time and time again) painter pants, a light blue oxford cloth dress shirt, and red, white, and blue suspenders my mother had given him the previous Christmas, never before this day worn. Phip's hot and sweaty hand in mine made us both feel sticky, yet bonded in some sort of mutually driven discomfort.

"Ah, and who is this beautiful young man?" asked a highly made up woman with a tight chignon, and a dramatic swoop in our direction.

Phip stood up to shake hands with her, but she grabbed both of his hands in hers and swirled him around. While she seemed to flow rather gracefully around and around, Phip clomped, side to side, eventually tripping over her extended right foot, landing roughly on his knees.

"Oops," she laughed, stopping to help him up. "You have such potential. Don't you think so too?" she asked, looking at me.

"Well, it seems that he wants to be in this show." I smiled. The room was rather warm, and I could see that many mothers and daughters had turned to look at us.

"That's nice," the woman said, avoiding my eyes, and looking back at Phip. "He has stature. He is blonde. He could be Apollo!"

"Who?" Phip asked.

"A great romantic part," she enthused, taking his hands, and holding them out. "Only for one as beautiful as you!"

"Mom?"

"What, honey?"

"Where's the bathroom?"

"Well, I'm not sure . . ."

"Boys have to go down to the second floor," said a mother close by.

"Lance? Lance? Where the devil are you," Phip's mentor shouted.

"Yea, what da ya want?" answered a tall, dark, handsome boy of about thirteen.

"Lance, darling, take this lovely boy to the bathroom downstairs, please?"

Lance looked at Phip, then turned and headed for the door.

"Follow him, I think," I mumbled to Phip.

While I waited for Phip to return (if ever), groups of six little girls were called into the rehearsal room to try out. In the *Nutcracker,* the opening sequence includes a scene with parents and children on Christmas Eve, and the children dance together at one point. I learned that there were fifteen shows all over the county, with three separate casts; but the boys were always used.

"Always?" I asked a mother with two little girls draped across her lap.

"They never can get boys interested. The girls get so disappointed when they don't make it. Say, does your son take dance?"

"No."

"Well, I think he'll have to take lessons in order to be in the *Nutcracker.*"

" Do other boys take dance lessons?" I asked.

"Sometimes. They are mostly the sons of dance teachers. Most of these boys have been in the *Nutcracker*

since they were toddlers. But your son is new blood."
Phip followed Lance closely back into the waiting
room, smiling from ear to ear, his pants a bit dishev-
eled.

"Phip," I called.

"What da ya want?" he answered.

"Everything O.K.?"

"We peed out the window into the street." he smiled.

"Boys, Boys!," the ballet mistress called. "It's time
for you to try out." The boys whooped and hollered
into the big room, and the door was closed behind
them.

After the tenth performance and the sixth bus ride
as a chaperone, the magic of the ballet was wearing
thin. However, Phip was thrilled that he got to stand
in as Clara's brother, the brat on stage who breaks her
nutcracker, a starring role of sorts. Otherwise nightly
and weekend afternoons up to and through the Christmas Holidays, Phip donned a velveteen suit, circa
1900, with a wide satin bow tie, and was smeared with
pancake makeup, rouge and eyeliner. Phip was in
thick with the other boys; I was relegated to ranks of
the other stage mothers of girls. The boys' mothers
were somehow involved in the production, either
dancing, directing, or some such. The soccer, basket-
ball, or tennis moms were all the horsey sort— rather
large, loud, and definitely bored. The *Nutcracker* mothers
were more fragile, lovely, and endlessly patient with
long rehearsals, and late performances, and curlers,
and such. We grew close as a group, and I felt sad that
I wouldn't be seeing this group of women, most of
whom were from different towns, for a long time, if

ever again, having no daughters myself.

"Did you enjoy the whole experience of the *Nutcracker*?" I asked Phip on the drive home after the last performance.

"It was O.K. Say, do I have to take those queer lessons anymore?"

"I thought you wanted to dance?"

"I just wanted to be in a big show and get applause."

"You know you could be Apollo some day?"

"Aw, mom, he's gay."

"Phip! That's not nice to say."

"That's what Lance says."

"Lance has been in a lot of *Nutcracker*'s."

"This is his last year, or else he says he's gonna run away."

"Well, Phip. I thought you did a great job. Really."

"Thanks, Mom. But I won't take any more of those lessons, O.K.?"

"Well, we'll talk about it tomorrow," I said, stifling a yawn.

Aliens

AFTER STOPS at the Elbow Room and George's Lounge, Frank ended up at the Green Room in the Hotel Allen. It was a small place with an R&B band and dancing. There were women, unattached, not like at the other places, and he had already psyched himself up by whispering, "Get laid. GET LAID." It made him feel better, voicing his obsession. It loosened the tight strap of anxiety at his chest, allowing cool, invigorating air to trickle in.

He went to the men's room, then to the bar, where he sat next to a sloe-eyed blonde who looked like his ex. She wore a chain and pendant that ended mid-cleavage—Here you go, get a load of this!

"Hello there," he said.

She didn't say anything.

"Is this seat taken?"

She raised her eyebrows. "What?"

"Is this seat taken?"

"I don't know."

"Well, I mean, did you notice anyone sitting here?"

The blonde didn't say anything, so Frank thought for a moment, figured she was a dead end. He ordered a Molson, headed down the bar a few seats, sat next to a thin brunette, who smiled, showed perfect teeth, and a healthy pink mouth bred of oranges and milk.

"Hello," she said.

Frank could swear he was tasting what she said. Her lips sparkled, the shine bouncing off mirrors and glasses, off his bottle of Molson. "Get laid," he whispered to himself. "GET LAID."

"I like this place," the brunette said.

"Oh, Jesus, yes, I like it too," Frank said.

"I like the band."

"Good R&B. Very good."

"Huh?"

"Rhythm & blues."

"I like fast music."

"Sure, jungle-like. Soothes the savage beast."

"Soothes?"

"The savage beast."

"Oh, I like that. I do."

The brunette was precious. She had a nice way of making everything seem fresh and joyous.

"What are you drinking there?" Frank asked.

"I like it."

"What is it?"

"Johnny gives it to me."

"Johnny?"

"Johnny!" The brunette called over to the bartender. "This man wants to know what this is."

"It's a strawberry daiquiri."

"Yes, please get her another," Frank said, then he turned to the brunette. "Isn't it too sweet?"

"I like it."

Johnny brought the daiquiri, and the brunette said thanks.

In fact, it was thank you for this, thank you for that; everything was nice. There wasn't anything she didn't like; but, on the other hand, there wasn't anything she knew about either. She didn't know Molson came from Canada; she didn't know what the term "Green Room" came from; maybe she heard of the Elbow Room and George's Lounge, but wasn't sure. Still, her smile was pure and magnetic. Frank liked how her teeth and tongue and lips all worked together.

The band struck up a new tune in the background. "Hey, what do you say, would you like to dance?"

They danced fast, the brunette without good balance, bumping against Frank and screeching whenever she did. Then, they danced a slow dance, she much thinner than she looked, shaking a lot, having trouble putting her feet where she wanted them to go.

"You haven't drunk too much already, have you?"

"I only have what Johnny gives me."

"Did you sneak a few before you came?"

"Oh, no, I can't drink in the house. Margaret won't let me ."

"Margaret?"

"She won't let me drink."

While they were talking, a short man came over, in a red sport coat, too large, his face chubby and his tongue sticking out.

"David," the brunette said, "Hi, David."

David waved, moved off without talking toward the band. He faced the dancers and the bar, began dancing by himself, unbalanced but freely, sort of like the brunette. "He's my friend," the brunette said. "He likes to dance. Wherever we go, he dances alone."

All of a sudden it struck Frank. "This Margaret, would I know her?"

"Oh, I don't know. I like Margaret."

"Do you like David?"

"I like David."

"Do you like to dance?"

"I like to dance."

"Is there any liquor in your drinks?"

"I like to drink."

"Excuse me, may I take you back to your seat?"

"I like to sit."

Frank followed her back to the bar. He watched her walk, the way she held her head, how she swung her arms. Even as she walked, she turned and smiled. Her mouth was gorgeous. He had never seen another mouth like hers, such beautiful teeth and lips.

After they sat, the brunette licked around the daiquiri glass, then playfully chewed on the strawberry ice crystals. On the dance floor, in front of the band, the brunette's friend, David, was dancing alone. His tongue was out, his balance was not good, but he was dancing freely.

"He likes to dance." the brunette whispered to Frank when she noticed him watching.

"Yes, I can see that. How does he get here?"

"Margaret brings him."

"And how do you get here?"

"My parents bring me to Margaret's, then she brings me."

"Is Margaret here?'

"Yes, she's with Jeanine. They're sitting over there."

The brunette pointed to a table not far from the dance floor, in a dark corner. Frank squinted, could see Margaret and Jeanine, waving. At the table there were three others— a tall man with suspenders, another short man, chubby face, tonque sticking out, and a very thin girl in an old plaid dress. They all waved.

Except for Margaret and Jeanine, even in the darkness of their table, it was obvious that they all had bad teeth, a physiological need not taken care of in their youth. The brunette was the exception. He had never seen one so pretty, with teeth like pearls.

"Get laid, right. That's what you ought to do, Frank." He was whispering to himself. "What you ought to do is go fuck *yourself*."

The brunette leaned over to him and said, "I like to whisper. My parents don't let me. But Margaret lets me whisper, whenever I want."

Aliens

SHE WATCHED HIM board the plane.

It was his silver covered bridge to someone, paid for by another. She waved to him as he walked away but he chose not to turn. She watched as others boarded, her face shadowed in the smoky Terminal window. Jimmy was sixteen. Now, he'd said, he could take care of himself.

The plane backed out of its space, coasted to a stop, and gathered a high pitched whine before its forward thrust. Her slender frame stood tall, watched, then turned slightly to follow the take-off. Two noisy toddlers took turns circling her legs, once each, before tumbling into empty chairs behind her. She smiled at their mother who shrugged her shoulders, shook her head, and called out in a tired voice for them to settle down.

She was tired, too. Looking back out the window, she watched his plane move farther and farther away. The night sky was filled with stars, satellites, and lights of the city, all reaching out like beacons. "Join us!" they called.

Her elbows leaned onto the forced air radiator just below the Terminal window; she focused on Jimmy's plane. It reminded her of the model she'd helped him build a few years ago—a light, somewhat unreal presence. Can it, could it, should it, will it actually ever fly? How would she carry on if Jimmy's plane crashed? She could sense the emptiness in her brain, the pressure in her chest. Her face flushed. The silence in her heart was a knife cut into her loneliness. Jimmy might not come back into her life as before. He was pulling away, stretching himself thinner and thinner between their worlds.

Jimmy's plane disappeared into the night. She walked the short distance to the crowded stand up bar to order a drink. Checking the time on her watch, she rolled her purse into her overcoat and tucked this bundle between her feet. Looking around she saw that there were no other women in sight. Usually car pools to scouts, skiing, or whatever were manned by moms. Where were all the girls gone off to now from here? First class with champagne and filet mignon? Here, it was smoky. There were many eyes seeing her even as the Celtics teased the Knicks. She was the Absolüt martini with a twist in a room full of Bud lights.

She finished her drink, paid for it, and walked down the fluorescent corridors to baggage claim and the main exit. She found a seat there near the revolving door which spun and spun around letting in and out swirls of air and travelers. She rested her chin upon the knees she tucked up and held onto tightly.

Outside, there were those who waited for their rides. There were taxis waiting for riders. In long-term parking, an elegant man wearing a Russian fur hat laid a bouquet of red roses on the hood of his VW and knelt to inspect his flat tire.

Superlative

JUANITA'S MOUTH was thin-lipped like Flo-Jo's, with smile creases in the corners. That was part of why he liked her; the rest he couldn't figure out exactly, except that she had soft, wavy hair, perfect teeth, and a body that appeared uncommonly healthy. And, she blushed— did black women blush? Her chocolate skin looked pinkish and smooth, and he had this need to touch her. If they were in a private place, he'd walk right over to her, raise his hand to her face, stroke her cheek.

She was sitting at a table working on adjectives, comparatives and superlatives: Good, Better, Best. Joanne, one of the other adult education teachers, had given her a worksheet, three columns to the page.

When she saw him looking over, she raised her hand.

"Hello, Juanita," he said when he got there. He sat down next to her.

"Well, hell-ooo."

"How are things going?"

She turned to him and smiled. "They are full up and moving in lots of directions, that's the way they are going."

He tried hard not to take a good look at her close up. He blinked an eye so he sort of saw her dimly, but it didn't help; her skin was soft and perfect, umblemished, and it indeed had pink color, shamelessly sensual.

"What can I help you with, Juanita?"

"Do you think you can help me?"

"Well, what've you got here?"

She smiled again, then pushed her worksheet over to him. "There," she said.

At first the page was a blur, because he caught her scent, caramel, clean and sweet. Her smell knocked him out, shutting down other senses, rattling around in his brain and chest and—Jesus God!—his scrotum was burning fire. And he had just sat down!

He closed his eyes for a moment and took a deep breath. Her worksheet came into view. The first column was the given word; the next two columns Juanita had filled in.

Adjective	Comparative	Superlative
GOOD	better	best
BAD	worse	worst
HAPPY	happier	happiest
BIG	biggier	biggiest
CUTE	cutier	cutiest

"Joanne got me started with the real tough ones," Juanita said. "She did GOOD and BAD and HAPPY, you know that bes' and wors' stuff."

"And you did the rest, Juanita?"

"No."

"No?"

"Alex Einstein did it." She laughed, breathed her sweet breath at him, and touched his arm.

"Juanita," he collected himself. "How'd he do, do

you think?"

"I'm not supposed to know, you're the teacher, isn't that right?"

"Well, if I'm doing a good job teaching, then—" He stopped; he wasn't going to get into pedagogy. It was stupid and bland and moribund. And she was sitting next to him, exuding her beautiful scent, being Juanita, smiling, showing herself off as she moved her neck, an arm, pulled back her shoulders. "Juanita, the first three are right, the ones Joanne got you started with: GOOD BAD, HAPPY. BIG is wrong."

"Oh, Jesus, wha's it suppose to be?"

"It's supposed to be: BIG, bigger, biggest."

"And what I got?"

"You got BIG, biggier, biggiest."

"Well . . . you big."

"I mean, Juanita, see the i there. There isn't supposed to be an i."

"No i, really?"

"Well . . . say the word for me. Let's try that."

"You want the word, you got it. That ain't no trouble."

He couldn't help smiling. "Juanita, you're something. You know that."

She smiled and moved closer. "You big and I likes him big."

"I'm sure you have someone bigger. I mean, there's got to be someone."

"You biggier."

"Bigger, Juanita."

"See, I knew that."

"Well, it doesn't have an i in it."

"What don't got no i?"

"Bigger."

"Then, you tell me this. How about cutier? You cutier."

"Juanita, I'm nothing of the kind."

"Does it got an i, has it?"

"No, it doesn't."

"Then, how do you say it?"

"Cuter. No i. You say it, Juanita."

"You cutier." She smiled.

And for a moment he felt he couldn't continue. He knew the rules of language; she knew nuance. He was frightened, imagined that he would lose control. She would sweep him off his feet, almost literally, and he would leave the classroom with her, walk, ride, loco-mote, until they found a place where they could lock in passion. She would brush her pink, chocolate cheeks up against his, kiss his eyes, pull his head to her breasts. Then, he would have to deliver. What would he have to do to satisfy this woman? She had bigger men, he was sure. Black men. Lots of them must be loving her. They were waiting for him to touch her. They would break his goddamn neck!

"Is that right?" she said.

"Is what right?"

"You cutier."

"It's, ah, cuter. SAD is sadder. BIG is bigger, not biggier. And so on. There's no i. The only time you use an i is when there is a y in the word.

"I ask'd why. I did, and you heard me."

"Juanita," he rolled his eyes and shook his head. "You are the cutiest. That's what you are. There's no argument."

"So don't be making me sadier by keeping teaching me and talking what I already know. Things be easier once you shut yourself up."

"Yes, I suppose they will," he said. "But, God, Juanita, having a dream come true can kill a man."

"Well, then, I'm jus' gonna get you readier and readier and more ready. Until you the readiest. What do you think on that?"

He looked at her and she was beautiful. He was going to pick up his hand and touch her face. But he looked around, saw the others in the class. He shook his head. It didn't help. He caught her scent once again, and it just rattled around and around, and he couldn't bear it, and wondered if he ever would. What was, he asked himself, what was the superlative of wonder?

Superlative

"*Y*OU MAKE the biggest deal out of everything," he snipped, his seventeen year old eyes squinting at me, thinking himself so right.

"You owe me fifty dollars," I said, coolly meeting his gaze.

"Some parents overlook a few dollars here and there. Not you!" He stood up and began to pace. "You know that I work hard as a dishwasher. Damned hard. Fifty bucks is about it for the week."

"It's your speeding ticket, sweety pie," I said.

"That's it! I'm out of here! Nag! Nag! Nag!" he yelled, pushing his chair hard.

There was nothing else to say. He slammed the side door and headed down to the driveway to burn some rubber on his way to Debbie's. Of course she'd understand. After all, he had promised to take her out to dinner at *The Mill* and fifty dollars was the ticket to ride. Only the best for Deb!

"Is it hamburgs again?" my younger son's disappointed voice whined, a deft cut into my reveries.

"Bix! Man, what's the big deal?"

"All we eat is hot dogs, hamburgs, some stew, some tuna and that kind of junk. Yuckiest!" He opened the refrigerator door, stared, then slammed it in disgust. "How about some fried chicken or steak or something else," he suggested, his voice a little less bratty.

"Don't yell at me, O.K.?" I could feel the tension build beneath my temples. I hate the dinner hours: Everybody taking out on everybody else the tensions of their days. On me. Bob still wasn't home from his trip. He'd expect us all to welcome him. Surprise! It's everyone for themselves, tonight.

"Mom, O.K. It's O.K. I'll fix scrambled eggs. Where's Simon?"

"He's probably at Debbie's," I sighed. "Or in the morgue," I thought.

"Debbie likes me best," Bix smiled leaning his elbows on the kitchen counter.

"I'd keep that news to yourself," I suggested.

"She said so!"

"Drop it, doll. I'll forget the hamburgs. You forget Debbie."

"Hey, can we go to the Pizza Palace?"

"You got any money?"

"Ah, Mom, you know I'm saving for a . . ."

"Forget it. Let me think."

Bix ran into the den to watch T.V.

"It's the *Dating Game* ," he yelled.

"In a minute!"

I called my best friend, Carol. She listened to me rant but forced me back to the realities of my life.

"You're trying to take care of everything. Bob's been gone a lot, and I'd guess the kids are afraid they're losing ground."

"We need to pull together, but instead, we're . . ."

"Just pull it together, then. God! kill them with kindness. Take them and even Debbie out to dinner. Use plastic. Hell, stop all the responsible stuff, and show them that you can be better than the challenges they put up; that you're one hell of a person sometimes, maybe even always.

"Well . . ."

"Just do it!"

"Bix!" I yelled into the den. Call Debbie's and see if Simon's there; then let me talk." Sim hated my calling her house—it always looked to him like I were hovering—a big, helium filled Petunia.

"He's on the phone," Bix called.

"Hi, Sim! It's me, Mom."

"Yea?"

"Sim? I have an idea."

"Jesus, Mom . . ."

"How about if you, me, Bix, and Debbie go out to dinner, my treat."

"What?"

"Say yes?"

"Mrs. Dean said I could eat with them."

"Please, Sim,—say, why don't you ask the Dean's, and I'll call Carol and . . ."

"Where would you go?"

"I don't know. How about *The Mill?*"

"Mom, no way! It costs . . ."

"Look Simon. I want to do this. Please?" I wiped my eyes on the back of my hand, glad the phone line separated us.

"Just a minute," he said.

I waited as Bix handed me a piece of paper towel for my nose.

"O.K! We're on!"

"Thanks, honey! This will be the greatest!"

"I'll pay you fifty next week," he whispered.

"I love you and Bix! You guys are the best kids, really." I handed the phone to Bix; "Tell Sim we'll meet him at *The Mill* in one hour."

"Hottest damn!" Bix shouted into the phone. "Prime rib, Simon."

Sex

SHE HAD FINISHED her shower; now he was taking his. That was their usual order, her first, then him. The bathroom, she felt, was her room in the house, under her control, and for him, thus, use of it required permission. She was dressing in the bed-room, and he was letting very hot water hit against the back of his neck, the water penetrating skin and muscle, stimulating him so he felt, again, the needful articula-tion of his genitals. His balls pulled close together, constricted with urgency, and his penis rose hard and unrelenting.

"Jesus Christ, Barbara," he yelled, "you've created a goddamn monster!"

There was nothing from her, so he yelled again, "Barbara!"

He heard her enter the bathroom. "What is it? What's the matter?" Then she pulled back the shower curtain, looked at him. "Holy Jesus!"

He didn't say anything, just looked down, head bent.

"How did that happen?" she asked playfully and reached out to touch him.

"Don't touch, Jesus!"

"Oh sure, then why'd you call?"

"Not to start anything. Just to show you. What the

hell is happening? It can't keep getting hard like this or I'll never be able to leave the house. I won't be able to do anything anymore."

"Suits me," she said. "You can be my sex slave." She reached out again, grabbed him.

"Jesus, I mean, you're almost dressed. It must be getting late."

"It's never too late."

He liked this about her: She was the aggressive one, wreaked havoc with all the myths of female propriety and decorum. She stepped out of her underpants, pulled her dress up, revealed herself. "Come on, drag ass, get out of there."

He turned the water off, was wet and dripping, began to reach for a towel.

"Come here," she said. She pulled the towel from him, bent over. "Come on, this way."

"But I'm wet. I'll get your dress wet."

"I want you wet. I want to feel you wet." She braced herself against the tile wall of the bathroom, rolled her ass at him, sensually, round.

He put the flat part of one hand on the small of her back, felt that little incuse arc of skin and muscle there. It felt good. Then he inched himself closer to her, his penis proud and pink, then got into her and pulled his stomach in because that needed to be done, then rocked back and forth, into her, out a little, farther into her, a soft stroke, a very hard, importunate one. She was already smooth and liquidy and warm, and because of this he was losing control, became abstracted by his sexual thrusts like a fervid, uninhibited little puppy.

It wasn't long, Barbara's hands slipped down from the tile, her ass arched higher, she contracted and moaned. He followed, rising as proud as a stallion, coming in a single strong exhalation.

"Holy, Jesus!"

"See, isn't that better?" she said, rising and turning to him.

He reeled back, leaned against the wall. "Better than what?"

She quickly reached out, cradled his balls. A little, twinkling drop of sperm came to the head of his penis, shone there like a dew drop. She put one fingertip to it, brought it to her mouth, her lips pursed, licked it. "Mmmm. Better than not," she said. Then she picked up and put on her panties, pulled down her dress, ruffled it out with her hands, looked in the mirror, touched a lock of hair.

God! the idea came over him, if she wanted to be unfaithful, it would only take minutes, as quickly as pulling up her dress and a lover stepping out of a shower.

But then he put the shower back on again, stepped in. As the hot water hit the back of his neck, it seemed he would once again have an erection, very soon. So where was love in all this, in this crazy period when all there was was sex, repeatedly?

She ripped open the shower curtain, startling him a bit. "See you, hon," she said. "I'm off to work. Mwa." She put a kiss on her hand, placed it on his chest, and then she was gone; he could hear her sweep through the living room and close the door.

"Mwa," he repeated, "Mwa."

As he took the soap to his genitals, washed them, he wondered how she would be able to go all day with his sperm inside her, with the feeling at any given moment in the day that she had just had sex.

"Mwa!" he screamed. "Mwa!" he kissed his hand, pressed it against an imaginary her. There had to be love here, along with his enslavement. There had to be.

Sex

THE FIRST THING I noticed about him was the way his bottom fit snuggly, compactly into his Levis. He stood there at the service desk, leaning slightly forward on the counter waiting for the manager. I put down the magazine I'd been thumbing through and took out a piece of gum from my purse. It was time to do some serious watching. First one of his rear cheeks, then the other tightened; he shifted his weight from his right foot, the left curled around in back, to both feet as the service manager approached. I saw that his bum was rounded from behind, but lean and straight on the sides. His thighs seemed firm, his jeans, fashionably worn. As the manager looked through a book of parts, my friend lit a cigarette, letting it rest between his lips while he knelt to tie a sneaker. Smoke swirled around the side of his face, his hand waving some of it away as he stood.

His hands were rough and broad, but expressive as he asked the manager some questions. His hands were working hands which would know just how to touch a girl so that she'd stay close and warm. These hands would know how to do a lot of things—patient hands that would wait for a response, but tease in the meantime. His hands could easily hold the steering wheel of a Porsche 911, or a customized GTI, or the Jag of my dreams. He had these hands and more—a body like a sleek, expensive chassis—a fast turbo charge with torque and a touch of velvet.

I picked up the magazine I'd been reading before, but this time to fan myself. I could feel beads of sweat tickle my armpits, and the hair just behind my ears. He finished his conversation with the service manager, ostensibly to wait, like me, for his own machine which would once again move below him, just for him. His car, no doubt a beauty like him—roadworthy, ready, relaxed, and well-buffed.

He sat next to me and reached into the pocket of his cotton shirt to retrieve another cigarette. Stirs of air from him to me carried scents of soap, spicy deodorant, and maybe some baby powder.

"Oooooooweeee," I sighed.

"What?" he asked, searching his pockets.

"Oh. Nothing. But, say, would you like a light?"

"Got one?"

I could feel his eyes on me as I searched my purse; with a hand that felt as if my fingers were tongs, I managed to light a match, and he inhaled deeply. He touched my hand as he blew out the match, his royal blue eyes holding mine through a waft of smoke. I stared, looking from one of his eyes to the other.

"Contacts," he grinned, flashing perfect teeth.

"Well, yes," I smiled back, blushing.

For a third time, I tried to focus on the magazine in my lap. Cars, vans, trucks, four-by-fours, and sporty jobs, all brand new with the shiniest of paint; and some really pretty girls with tousled blond hair lolled about the doors or hoods seeming to call out to hunky guys behind the wheels—"Hey, babe, I'm *impressed !!*" He, of course, would stay cool. After all, he could drive over to the next page for another chick if this one didn't work out. I could smell the new leather of the interiors, smooth and tight to the touch, a touch of class. His hands would lightly hold the small, neat steering wheel—we had earlier climbed into the two-seater-sporty one. I closed my eyes and thought, Take me away, to feel windblown and free.

I came to as he shook my arm.

"Bob, there, the manager, says your bug is ready," he said. His eyes were blue as an Indiana summer sky, his breath fresh and warm.

"Want to go for a ride?" I whispered.

Phone

He WAS ALWAYS tired when he came home, and this evening was no different. He was a public school assistant superintendent with the responsibility for four hundred fifty faculty, their curriculum, evaluation, all the little eccentricities that their life in pedagogy brought to them. Then, he wasn't home but an hour, and he often had to go out again, for a meeting with parents, school board, civic leaders.

And—the more tired he got, the more she used the telephone as a weapon.

He pulled into the drive, noticed the kids' bicycles were out, and other bicycles belonging to neighbor kids. It upset him, all those bicycles thrown this way and that, bending the hedge, in the flower bed, one in the middle of the drive. He got out of the car, began to move the bicycle in the drive, then just decided to leave it there, and to leave the car where it was.

When he got in, she was on the phone.

"Jerry, I don't believe it." She was talking to her cousin in Nebraska. "I don't believe it."

It seemed, over the telephone, there was very little she believed.

Then, there was a scream from upstairs, and a crash.

As he ran to the stairs, he was greeted with a was-tepaper basket tumbling down, spilling napkins, bathroom trash. This relaxed him in a strange way; it was just an object tumbling, inert, non-metabolizing.

His daughter appeared at the top of the stairs, and behind her three of her little friends.

"Maryann did it," his daughter said. "She threw it."

"She told me to," Maryann said.

"Well, whoever did it, be careful, don't do it anymore. And come down and pick it up. Now."

"I'm not going to do it. It wasn't me," one of Maryann's friends said.

"It wasn't me either," another said.

He bent over, picked up the basket, then turned in the direction of the phone.

"I don't believe it." She was talking with the same tone of voice, the same posture. When she saw him, she said matter of factly, "Jerry, Frank's home."

"The kids are going crazy," he said.

"Jerry, excuse me. Just a minute." She held her hand over the mouthpiece. "Did you say something, Frank?"

"The kids are throwing things down the stairs. There's bicycles in the drive. I almost drove over one."

"Excuse me, Frank. I'm on the phone." She turned back to the telephone with a smile. "No, Jerry. No problem. Ahuh . . ."

He went upstairs, picking up spilt tissue, other bathroom trash, dropping them into the basket. Upstairs, behind his daughter's bedroom door, the children were playing music, singing along with Madonna. The door was open just a crack. He peeked in. Everyone was on the bed, dirty shoes and sneakers on, holding brushes, combs, singing into them. His daughter saw him, jumped off the bed. "You can't look, daddy. This is private." She shut the door. To the closed door, he said, "Take your shoes off if you want to get on the bed." But there was no response.

At least I'm trying to keep things going, he thought. He went into his bedroom. She's into denial, into escaping by goddamn telephone. He looked at the bedroom extension on the night stand. He resisted the idea of picking up the receiver, screaming into her ear.

He took off his suit, put on a t-shirt and jeans. He'd have to eat, shower, shave, dress-up again; tonight was a school board meeting. But for the time being he'd be comfortable. Relax.

"Hi,Dad!" His son bumped into him at his bedroom door.

"Hi, Eric!"

"What are we having for supper? I'm hungry."

"Me too, Eric. I'm hungry too."

"Pizza, Dad. What do you say, we have pizza?"

"I have a meeting tonight, Eric. I don't have time to cook one with you guys."

"Great! Then we can go to Pizza Hut. Huh, Dad?"

"In the pants on the bed, Eric. Take a twenty. You and your sister—see if your mom will take you. Include your sister's friends, if their parents let them."

"All right. Hey!"

He began to descend the stairs. He could not hear his wife on the telephone anymore, but then it rang, she picked it up. "Hello. . . Yes. . . Okay. . ."

When he got downstairs, the phone was off the hook; she was primping in front of the hall mirror.

"Adjusting your ear?" he asked.

"Oh, Frank . . . It's for you."

"Can't be."

"Then it's not." She walked past him, up the stairs.

He heard his son telling her about Pizza Hut, then his bedroom door closed, and his son's voice behind it.

He looked at the telephone receiver. It looked foreign to him. "Yes?" he said tentatively.

"Frank, Jesus! This is Bob. I've been trying to get you for the last hour."

"Something wrong, Bob?"

"You've got to handle that bid on the ramps for the handicapped. And the new bus route. I left those items on my desk. I didn't have time to get to them."

"They're on your desk, Bob?"

"Hell, Frank, you're only a couple miles away. Run over, get them, put on a quick study before the meeting. That'll be good enough. See you half an hour early, so you can brief me. See you, Frank. See you."

"Goodbye, Bob," he said, but Bob had already hung up. He set the receiver back down, still had his hand on it when it rang again.

"Frank."

"Yes."

"While you're at the office, pick up one of those overheads. We can put the bus route on that."

"Bob?—"

"See you, Frank. See you." He hung up.

Put the route on the overhead?—he'd need to make transparencies. Or were they for the opaque? In business they were all called view-graphs, and they didn't use them anymore. Graphs—he hated the entire concept. On them a good idea looked bad, a bad idea good. To do anything, he'd have to hurry. Damn it, Bob! Son-of-a-bitch!

He ran upstairs, turned the corner in the hall, caught his little daughter with an elbow to the forehead just

as she opened the door to her room. He felt the small-
ness of her skull, the thin, smooth skin of her scalp. She
fell to the floor.

"Daddy, ohhh."

"Oh, Katherine. Jesus, honey, I'm sorry."

Her friends came out of her room, stood there, stared
at him.

"Ohhh, daddy." Her daughter was holding her forehead. It was red, beginning to swell.

"Oh, Jesus, Katherine. I'm so sorry."

Eric appeared in the hall. "What'd you do, Dad? Did
you knock Katherine out?"

"Eric, get me a cold washcloth, okay . . ."

Katherine began to cry, little tear drops falling slowly
down her cheeks.

"Eric, go get it. Get the fucking washcloth!"

Eric winced, Katherine's little friends shrunk back
into her room, Katherine began screaming. In his bedroom, he could swear he heard his wife on the extension. "Peg," she was saying to her single friend in New
York, "I don't believe it. I don't believe it."

Phone

$\mathcal{H}$E REACHED THE PHONE booth about two seconds ahead of me. We had been neck and neck, he from one direction and me from the other; his weight slowed him down, but my flip flops gave him the final edge. Shit. Chivalry was dead. Again.

I heard him drop in several coins as I sat on the curb. Maybe he'd be quick. There seemed to be no need for my getting all hysterical. Bill could wait a little longer for my call; if he didn't, then . . . Geesus! I hoped this bull would finish fast.

"Hi, honey, it's me," he said.

Pause.

"Have the kids noticed I'm gone?" he continued, leaning way into the phone, his bulk slopping onto the phone's counter, his elbows resting on the metal walls in back of the phone. His knit shirt was pulled up above some flesh rolls, the rim of his underpants peered above his khakis.

There were some "uh huhs," and some "ummms," and "yea's?"

I stood up. I thought he needed to know that I was waiting; so I coughed, and paced around, and rattled the change in my pocket. He looked at me from under a meaty arm, only to go back into his full phone press, and dive into his pants pocket for more change. Clink.

Along with my wait, his underpants line broadened.
"What did you have for supper?" he asked.

"Who the fuck cares," my brain screamed.

I sat back down on the curb and picked up a stick.
I wrote "Bill" in the sandy dirt next to the curbing and
circled his name with a heart. It would have been so
much easier if I could have called him from home, but
no: Too many ears and noses there. Too many vows
hanging around home like so many poisoned arrows—
a gothic and painful game of "Gotcha!" The next phone
was a mile up the road; next time, I promised myself,
I'd wear my sneaks. "Lord," I thought. "It's been fifteen minutes. I'd said that I was just going out to walk
around the block. No big deal. Except Roger might get
worried and come looking for me. Maybe I was just
flattering myself. Anyway, Bill needed to hear from me
that we could get together tomorrow. YES, YES, YES,
my brain screamed—but Bill couldn't hear me because
of this phone yoyo here."

"Maybe you could drive up to see me? Ralph told
me that you can see four states from Mt. Greylock," he
said. He was now turned sideways, his right foot
extended behind him in sort of a runner's stretch
position. "You could leave the kids at my mother's and
drive up tomorrow night. My room's got a nice double
bed . . ."

Pause.

He began to tap his foot up and down on the sidewalk just outside the phone booth.

It seemed so sad. People separated by jobs or other
commitments or whatever, wanting to stay connected.
He and I, this summer's evening, needing the phone.

"You can't?" His anguished voiced sounded beyond the booth.

"You bitch," I thought about his wife, the mother of his children—What was more important? Routine, or a needy mate? But not even I could answer this dilemma. For some time, neither had appealed to me. If Roger had called me in such a way? Early on I would have rushed to his side; but he never called. Now? I'd not be home.

He hung up the phone, finally. I could see that he wiped his eyes, then tried to hike up his pants, his oversized belly an immovable force in the opposite direction.

"Sorry," he said to me, shuffling along the sidewalk, heading up the street.

"No problem," I answered.

Although I claimed my space inside the phone booth, I watched him move along, then stop by a Ford Escort, and squeeze into it. "Poor, lonesome guy," I thought. "Let him be luckier the next call he makes."

I dropped in a dime and dialed Bill's number. This call would have to be quick. Lord knew I'd had enough time to walk around the block a few hundred times by now.

Ring. Ring.

"God damn, Bill. Please be there."

Landings

His small office was crowded with book-cases and files and a table strewn with pencils, calculator slips, computer printouts. He was at his desk, and although it was late Friday, the end of his work week, he was, nevertheless, in deep concentration, immersed in his work.

Margarite, his secretary, came to the doorway. "That's enough for me. I've got Joan and her boyfriend coming by. Remember, I told you, I'm cooking and inviting Laura and her husband over."

He raised his head. "What's that?"

"I said I'm leaving."

"Oh, sure, uhuh. Where're you going?"

"Home. I'm going home."

He jotted down some notes on a slip of paper. "Is it that late already?"

"Yes, it's that late. I should have left earlier." She waited for a response, but he just stared, glassy-eyed. Finally, she said, "You've got one of your honeys waiting outside."

"What?"

"You have a visitor."

"Do you know who it is?"

"You're the one making these appointments, not me. She's female, no surprise. Did you jot anything down on your desk calendar?"

He glanced at his desk calendar, was staring blindly.

"Here, let me help you. Friday, the fourteenth. Should be the thirteenth for all the luck I'm having. No oyster mushrooms. The recipe calls for them specifically. My entire lunch wasted, looking everywhere. Here. The young lady is Nadine. Nadine who, if you don't mind my asking?"

"She's the new itinerant in art. She's got the elementary schools."

"Single or married? If it makes a difference nowadays. She's not wearing a ring."

"She's got ideas for bringing artists from Cummington into the schools."

"Yes, I'm sure she's got ideas."

"Margarite, Jesus, you'll never change."

"Neither will females looking for a man. Her week ended at 3:00, but she's so dedicated, she's still around. Sure, aha!"

The phone rang, muted on his desk, quite loud outside the doorway on Margarite's desk.

"It's the phone," he said.

"So answer it, I'm leaving."

He reached over, answered, "Hello, The Berkshire Schools. This is the Assistant Superintendent's Office . . . Hi Cassie! Hi, hon! How's daddy's girl? . . . Ahum . . . Yes . . . Sure." He put his hand over the phone. "It's Cassie."

"Say hello for me." Then Margarite pointed out the door. "Remember, you've got one waiting. Now, I'm out of here."

The phone still to his ear, he rose, watched Margarite walk the length of the office, turn the corner, disappear. Nadine, the art teacher, was in the waiting room, reading a magazine. She saw him, lowered the magazine, smiled. Jesus, she was stacked! He pointed: I'm on the phone. She nodded, aha, jiggled her tits.

"Ahem . . . yes . . . when your mommy leaves for New York, she can drive by my apartment and you can stay over until she returns . . . sure . . . simpler to put her on . . ."

He waited, watched Nadine reading again. She had big eyes, very attractive. Finally, the voice of his ex came through, shrill, as usual.

"Yes, I'm alone. Margarite's gone for the day . . . yes . . . no . . . anytime after noon . . . I said *after* noon . . . Jesus, because no reason, except you said you're not going until two . . . ."

He closed his eyes, waited. It was a long time before he spoke again.

". . . At eleven then . . . You tell Cassie . . . No, I lied, I can't talk, I've got someone waiting . . . You're wrong, male . . . business . . . Why would I? It makes no difference . . . And my goodbye to Cassie."

He set the phone down. It felt heavy, like lead. He rubbed his arm, rolled his shoulder. All of a sudden he was so tired. He took a deep breath, then exhaled, as long as he could.

Nadine—what a beautiful name. She was young, vibrant, and in this new world, as he was beginning to confirm, vitality was a transferable quality, from one sex to another. He ran his fingers through his hair, loosened his tie.

"Nadine," he called out.

"Yes, Mr. Thompson."

"It's Frank, Nadine. Call me Frank."

She smiled widely.

"Now, tell me," he said, "what's on your mind?"

Landings

*W*HEN WE SPLIT, Bob took "his" boat, *Bobbin*, and I kept the old summer cottage, *Landings*, which had been in my family for generations. Chip and I had spent the summer there patching roof leaks and loose shingles; but in the evenings we'd sit down by the dock wrapped in old sweaters and watch the light show—lit boats whooshing along, Japanese lanterns on other docks, the amusement park way way down the lake, and the stars and moon moving on the mirror of the lake. We'd talk, or rather Chip would talk about girls, boats, "Nessie," video games, a movie last seen, and the rules of hockey. I knew he was tired, his eyes wide, his sitting on the edge of his chair, afraid to sit back, to give in to the damp, lapping night. Finally he'd shiver and yawn, making sort of a croaking sound, and his verbal momentum would interrupt itself.

Bob had left mid-summer as no surprise. Each year since my mother's death, the joys of sharing a summer cottage by the water had waned—we just didn't care to entertain each other anymore. Chip missed Bob and his "I don't give a damn" ways. I took things like kitchen messes and wet towels under the bed seriously—but never people, and never for long. I missed Bob more for what he did at the cottage, like maintenance, than his personality. Now that it was almost fall, I knew that the closing up of the cottage for the winter would be an enormous hassle. There were shutters to close and nail, a chimney to seal, water to shut off, dry linens and towels to store in plastic bags, and all the generic sweaters and blankets to be folded in the cedar chest. I wasn't sure yet whether Bob would help me with the dock. Maybe I should just pay someone to reel it in, section by section. Perhaps the main issues all along were personal independence. *Landings* was certainly a crash course: Haven and headache, childhood nostalgia mixed with grown up grief, and the ever leaking roof. I wasn't sure it was worth it, this demanding hideaway. It was more a question of who would carry on the family traditions. There wasn't much family left. Friends? I wasn't yet sure exactly who might stay, mine or Bob's.

Our last night at the cottage, Chip and I sat huddled together on the bench by the dock, a lantern near our feet. We had worked all day, gone out to dinner, took our showers, and prepared for the cold night. But it was our ritual to say goodnight to the world and our thoughts dockside. We sat together, wrapped in a blanket, hot cider in our thermos. The lake blew choppy with fickle winds, almost at once in our faces, or down our necks. There were no boats out, but the lights still glittered up and down the shores.

"When I was a little girl spending some of my summers here with my Grandma, I wanted so much to be able to fly over the lake to see the lights from above." I mused.

"Mom? Do you know how to land a remote control plane?"

"Is this going to be a long story?"

"I don't know."

"Well, maybe we should go . . . "

"It's really amazing, Mom. See, it's like this . . ."

"Don't wiggle too much, Chip. I'm freezing!"

"I've gotta show you a little."

"O.K. Just move the story along, O.K? Otherwise, we'll fuse right to this bench and be here forever, or at least until it gets warm again, and then maybe "Jaws" will find us . . ."

"Mom! C'mon. Listen."

"I'm sorry. Shoot."

"Well, see, it's real hard to land a remote control plane because your main lever is not as flexible as would be the real steering device on the plane. But anyway, you've got this box thing and there are a couple of buttons and the lever. There is no sound because the pilot has to concentrate on the directions from below. So it gets real tense. You pull the lever down just a little because if you pull it too much, the plane will crash. But you do it easy, and then let the plane stabilize at its new level before pulling it down again. The other thing is that you don't want to scare the people on the plane, or have them fall out. "So," he said, using one hand to demonstrate the plane, "the plane lowers and lowers, a little bit at a time, easy does it, circling slowly, but not too slowly or it will drop out of its pattern. By tilting the lever, the plane turns, then lowers, then flattens to hold tight. Too much wind will crash it, so you must never fly in a lot of wind. Anyway, you don't want the plane to take off too fast on the ground because it can fall over and you can lose a wing. So the trick is to finally turn off the power, and let the plane plop onto the runway, and then it just stops." Chip was silent, staring off across the lake.

"That's it?" I asked.

"It's hard, Mom, really."

"Oh, I'm sure it is; It's just that I thought the landing would somehow be more complex. That you'd talk longer."

"That's it!"

As we walked back up to the cottage, that night, I decided that we'd be back next season. After all, a remote control plane and its pilot are much like a place and its people, surviving the bumps.

About the authors:

PAUL MILENSKI *and* MARILYN GRANDE *have been writing fiction independently until this collaboration. Between them they have published over one hundred fifty stories, won AWP, PEN Syndicated, and Transcript Writing Competitions, and have been translated into Italian, Spanish, German, Japanese, and Chinese. Both received graduate degrees from U-Mass, Amherst. Paul was also educated at Middlebury, North Adams State, and the University of Iowa's Writer's Workshop; Marilyn, at Miami University of Ohio and Indiana University. Paul is a former laborer and school administrator, now a full-time writer living in Pittsfield, MA. Marilyn, a former swimsuit model, is an Albany, NY, school psychologist. They are completing another book together and have plans for more.*